Filthy Boss

Filthy, Volume 1

Amy Brent

Published by Amy Brent, 2021.

FILTHY BOSS

First edition. March 1, 2021.

Copyright © 2021 Amy Brent.

ISBN: 979-8201899004

Written by Amy Brent.

Also by Amy Brent

Filthy
Filthy Boss
Filthy Doctor
Filthy Professor
Filthy Seal
Filthy Cowboy
Filthy Daddy
Filthy Coach

Forbidded
The Doctor's Fake Marriage

Forbidden
Fake Fiance
One More Chance
Crave Me
My Best Friend's Dad
The Doctor's Fake Marriage
Dad's Best Friend

Forbidden Fantasies
Daddy's Business Partner
Daddy's Friend
Daddy O
Climbing His Corporate Ladder
Taken By Daddy's Boss
Filthy Liar

Standalone
Teachers' Pet
Filthy Box Set
Knocked Up By My Brother's Best Friend
My Best Friend's Brother
My Best Friend's Ex
Say You're Mine
Club Desire Box Set
My Boyfriend's Dad
Fighting For Her
Forbidden Love Box Set
Love Undercover
Friends With Benefits
A Royal Menage
Baby Fever
Vegas Baby
Brother's Best Friend for Christmas
Christmas With My Best Friend's Dad
My Son's Sitter
Single Dad's Christmas Present
Surrendering To 3 Alphas

Because I Love You
Catching Up With Daddy
Claiming Cinderella
Double Trouble
First Love
First Time
Knocked Up By My Brother's Best Friend
My Best Friend's Boyfriend
Pretend Daddy
Redemption
Roomies With Benefits
Royally Yours
Rub Me The Right Way
Show Stopper
That One Night
The Baby Contract
Truth Or Dare
Santa's Naughty List
Quickie on Christmas
Con Man

Table of Contents

FILTHY BOSS

by

AMY BRENT

CANDICE CARLSON:

Men are douchebags! I'm sorry, but there's just no other way to put it and they can't deny it. They only want one thing from us, girls. Then, just as you're about to give it to them, they dump you like a hot rock because their mommy says you're not good enough for their little boy. Seriously, bitch? I'll show you not good enough with my fist in your nose.

Then I get assigned to work for Tanner Wright, the bad boy billionaire CEO who thinks his money, good looks, and big bulge in his jeans can get him whatever he wants. And what he wants at the moment is to get into this girl's pants. What he doesn't know is, that's a place where no man has gone before.

The guy's a billionaire douchebag and I'm a reluctant virgin. That combination could make for a very interesting workplace, indeed.

TANNER WRIGHT

It's a lot of pressure, living up to a reputation like mine. You just try being a billionaire bad boy CEO for a week and see how you handle things. I'll bet you end up in the press more than I do!

When you have the looks, money, charm, and bedroom skills that I have, the world is your oyster. So many mansions to buy, exotic cars to drive, yachts to captain, and so many women to... well... you know what the ladies want from Mr. Wright.

So, when Candice Carlson is assigned to work on a project for my company, it's only fitting that I give her a shot at the brass ring. She's young and brilliant and beautiful. And there's something mysterious about her that draws me to her like a moth to a flame.

She can try to resist all she wants, but when Tanner Wright wants something, you can bet the bank that he will get it; one way or another.

CHAPTER ONE: Candice Carlson

I was sitting at my desk munching on a take-out salad from the cafeteria downstairs, when the email from my boss came through. I glanced at the large computer monitor sitting to my left, but didn't bother opening the email. I already knew what it was.

I had been expecting the email since earlier in the day when my boss told me that our company, Goldman & Stern Management Consultants, had won a ten-million-dollar management consulting contract with Wright Enterprises, and that I would be one of the management consultants on the team.

I chewed a mouthful of lettuce and leaned over to read the subject line: *Confirmation of Meeting Scheduled with Tanner Wright at Wright Enterprises.*

I clicked the link that would automatically add the meeting details to my electronic schedule and went back to eating my salad.

A year ago, I would have been jumping up and down at the thought of meeting with billionaire entrepreneur, Tanner Wright, and his team. Now, this would be just another in a long line of boring meetings with rich douchebags who used Goldman & Stern's management consultants – like me—to do their dirty work.

Wow, sometimes I was amazed at how tarnished I had become in just one short year at Goldman. I don't remember what I expected this job would be, but this wasn't it.

Still, it was better than slaving away at a non-profit for twenty-grand a year. That was more fulfilling, but this allowed me to buy a lot cooler stuff.

I sighed as I stabbed a cherry tomato and bit it in half with my front teeth. I had already Googled Tanner Wright in anticipation of the meeting. Not that I didn't already know who he was. Everyone in business knew who Tanner Wright was because he was the stuff of legend.

Thirty-five years old, single, tall, dark, and handsome; with the build of an athlete and the brain of a Rhodes Scholar.

He started Wright Enterprises as a little computer fix-it service in his parents' basement fifteen years ago, and the company did six billion in revenue last year.

Wright was in to everything now: from computing to networking to cyber-security software to fiber optics. But it took more than generating a ton of revenue for a guy to impress me these days. In my mind, I already had him pegged as just another billionaire playboy who thought he could buy the world and everyone in it.

I took a sip of the watery iced tea that came with the salad and looked out the twentieth-floor window at the hazy Chicago skyline.

"I'll bet he's a major douchebag," I heard myself say.

I couldn't help it.

Whenever I thought about men these days the word "douchebag" automatically came to mind.

In fact, the word "douchebag" was becoming synonymous with the word "man" in my mind.

Man, douchebag.

Douchebag, man.

Call me jaded, but in my mind, they were one and the same.

I took another bite of the lettuce and munched as I sighed. Why do men have to be such douchebags, I wondered. Aren't there any good men left in the world? Surely, they're not *all* gay or married.

Okay, maybe I'm exaggerating just a little bit. Maybe not all men on planet earth are douchebags. Maybe it's just the males of the species that I have personally met over my twenty-four years on the planet were douchebags.

They didn't all start out that way, of course. Some of them were perfectly nice in the beginning. They seemed to evolve into douchebags after they met me. Maybe that was it. Maybe I was the common denominator. Maybe I took perfectly nice guys and turned them into total douchebags. I was patient zero!

I licked the dressing from my lips and reached for the tea. Maybe that was my special power, I thought. I had the power to turn perfectly nice guys into douchebags.

Nah. Who am I kidding.

I don't have special powers.

Men are quite capable of becoming douchebags all on their own.

They certainly didn't need any influence from me.

The most recent douchebag in my life was my ex-boyfriend, Scott, who dumped me after dating for five years because his mother didn't think I was good enough for him.

He actually said those words to me.

"I'm sorry, Candice, but Mother doesn't think you're good enough for me."

"I'm not marrying your mother, Scott," I shot back. "The question is, what do you think?"

The prick didn't hesitate. He looked me dead in the eye and said, "I think Mother is probably right."

And with that, he turned and walked out the door and never looked back.

I was like, are you kidding me, mother f*cker?

I've dated your douchebag ass since freshman year at college, saved my virginity for our wedding night, and two months before the wedding, I'm not good enough for you?

Seriously?

F*ck you!

And f*ck your mother!!!

I felt my cheeks getting hot. Even though it's been over a year since Scott dumped me, it still makes me fume.

Granted, I didn't come from money like Scott's family did. The Carlson family was lower middle class at best, but I worked my ass off to get through college and then graduate school. I graduated with an MBA from Harvard last year and was recruited by Goldman & Stern to join their management consulting group before the ink on my diploma was dry.

I have a windowed-office in a Chicago high-rise, and pulldown one-fifty a year plus bonuses. I have a killer apartment downtown, and am on the fast track to make partner within five years. And I'm not good enough for your piece of shit son?

Again, dear mother, f*ck you!

I frowned at my own thought. I never used to cuss like this. Granted, this conversation is only going on in my head, but now I have the vocabulary of a drunken sailor.

And I blame it on Scott and his mommy.

Scott said his mommy thought I was a bad person. She didn't like the way I treated her little boy.

Fine. Whatever. Sure, I can be a little abrasive at times, and maybe I bossed Scott around a bit, but come on, the guy could barely wipe his own ass without mommy's help.

If he didn't have me telling him what to do he would have spent most of his days bouncing through life like a pinball.

Not good enough for your son.

F*ck you, you old bat.

Your son wasn't good enough for me!

I chewed on a chunk of lettuce and scolded myself for even thinking about this stuff. I mean, it had been over a year since I last saw Scott. Why was this still sticking in my craw?

And why didn't I want anything to do with men in general now?

Had Scott scarred me for life?

Was I destined to be an old maid?

Or maybe a lesbian?

Hmm, no, I didn't swing that way.

At least not yet...

I was young, healthy, and horny as the next girl. The fact that I was still a virgin irked me a bit. After all, the whole "saving myself for Mr. Right" crap flew out the window the day Scott dumped me. I'd jump Mr. Wrong's bones if given the chance.

It's not that I haven't had opportunities to have sex. Jesus, you can't walk down the hallway here at Goldman & Stern without running into a swinging dick. It's just that I don't want to be bothered by a man at this point in my life.

And as I said, men are douchebags.

I'd never had a cock inside of me, so maybe I didn't know what I was missing. But I had long, nimble fingers and the foot-long vibrating dildo I bought online that I called "George Clooney". George was always waiting for me in my nightstand. What the heck did I need a man for?

No, better for me to focus on my career rather than my love life. I was only twenty-four. I still had plenty of time left on the old biological clock, although some days I could hear it ticking louder than others.

I had my entire future all mapped out. I would find a man after I made partner, probably when I was thirty or so, squeeze out a couple of cute babies by the time I was thirty-five, and find a nice French nanny to raise them for me while I went back to work.

A solid plan, if I do say so myself.

Why would I let a man screw that up?

I finished the salad and wiped the dressing from my lips, then clicked on the email to find out when I'd be meeting with Tanner Wright, who I knew would be a douchebag, albeit a douchebag worth billions of dollars.

CHAPTER TWO: Tanner Wright

"I don't give a damn what it costs, Barry! Just buy the fucking thing! And stop calling me every five seconds. If you miss out on this deal because you're on the phone with me, I'll rip off your balls and feed them to my Doberman! Now go!"

I slammed down the phone and balled my hands into fists. I shook them at the ceiling and growled. "Christ, why does everything have to be so fucking hard?"

Henry Costas, my best friend of ten-years and Executive Vice President of Business Development at Wright Enterprises, sat on the other side of my desk with a mild look of concern on his pleasant face.

"Is there a problem?"

I shook my head at him. "I sent my car guy out to the Barrett-Jackson auction in Vegas to bid on a 1961 Ferrari 250 in mint fucking condition, and he's calling me every ten seconds to update me on the bids. I'm like, for Christ sake, just buy the fucking thing!"

"What was the last bid?" Henry asked.

"Fifteen million," I snapped. "The catalog estimated that it could go as high as twenty-five million and I'm like, just fucking bid twenty-five million, Barry, and get it over with! I don't understand the problem."

I caught Henry grinning at me. When we met, I was in grad school at MIT and he was my business management professor. I didn't have twenty-five cents to my name back then, and here I was a decade later throwing a temper tantrum over a twenty-five-million-dollar car that I would probably never drive.

"Billionaires do have their own particular sets of problems, don't they?" Henry said with a sigh.

He crossed his legs and brushed lint from his knee. Henry wasn't a billionaire, but he'd gotten rich when Wright Enterprises went public five years ago. He could have easily spent twenty-five million dollars on a car, but he would never do so because he felt it was an overindulgence and a complete waste of money.

I remember him asking me once, "Why buy a fifty-thousand dollar Rolex when a fifty-dollar Timex tells the same time?"

My answer, of course, was, "Because a fifty-dollar Timex won't get you laid!"

The truth was, I had more money than I could ever hope to spend. Wright Enterprises was now one of the largest conglomerates in the world, with business holdings in practically every country on the planet.

I had made billions of dollars and could buy anything and anyone I wanted. And at the moment, I wanted that fucking Ferrari GT!

"We need to talk about the Anderson acquisition," Henry said as the humor melted from his face. That was Henry. Enough frivolity! Back to the salt mines!

He reached into the briefcase that was sitting next to his chair and brought out a thick folder detailing our impending acquisition of Anderson Telecommunications, a regional telc0 in Arizona that had fallen on hard times.

We were going to acquire Anderson for pennies on the dollar. We'd either fix it if we could or tear it apart if we couldn't.

It would be our first foray into telecommunications, so Henry was edgy. And rightfully so. I paid him to worry about such things so I didn't have to.

"Is there a problem with the acquisition?" I asked, watching him balance the folder on his knee. He set a pair of reading glasses on the tip of his nose and opened the folder. He removed the first page and looked down his nose at it.

"I'm looking to prevent problems," he said, sliding the page across the desk at me. "As we discussed, since this is our first telecom acquisition and neither of us are experts in the industry, I thought it would be a good idea to get an expert set of eyes to look over

Anderson's financials and interview the management team before we signed the final deal."

I kept a red rubber ball sitting on my desk. It was supposed to be a stress ball, you know, a rubber ball you squeeze whenever you're feeling stressed. The truth was, I rarely felt stressed. But I had the attention span of a tsetse fly and if I wasn't constantly doing something with my hands, I had a hard time paying attention.

I squeezed the ball in my left hand and picked up the sheet of paper in my right. It was a letter of engagement from Goldman & Stern, the company who would handle this part of the due diligence.

I held out the paper and summed up my take on it. "So, we're going to pay Goldman & Stern ten million dollars to do the due diligence on Anderson? Tell me again why we can't do all the due diligence in-house? Why isn't our corporate legal department handling this?"

"We are doing the lion's share of the due diligence in-house," Henry said. "But as I said before, some details that are specific to the telecom industry are out of our wheelhouse. Paying G&S ten-million to uncover skeletons in closets and mistakes on balance sheets is money well spent."

I wouldn't hesitate to spend twenty-five million on a car, but hated wasting a dime when it came to my business. It was mostly a formality because the acquisition was pretty much a done deal, but Henry was a stickler for covering our asses and I was grateful for it.

I scanned through the project description and a list of the people who would be doing the work. I sailed the paper across the desk at him, then leaned back in my chair and tossed the ball into the air.

I said, "Fine, whatever you think is best. Do you know anyone on the team Goldman is sending over?"

Henry picked up the paper and set it on top of the folder. He peered down through the glasses at the list of names. He ran a finger down the list. "Yes, the senior people I've worked with before. Stan Robbins and Juliette Ruiz. Bob Gaines and Irving Hunt I know by reputation. I don't now recognize this last name. She must be new. Candice Carlson."

"I've never heard of Candice Carlson either," I said. I caught the ball and tossed it into the air again. "Did they send her resume?"

Henry opened the folder and wet his finger to fan through the pages. "I have resumes on the key players. Let's see... Candice Carlson. BA from Penn, MBA from Harvard. Graduated with honors last year."

"Fresh meat," I sighed.

Henry ignored me and kept reading. "She joined Goldman right out of Harvard, so she has to be top notch. She has been on several teams that have consulted for Goldman in the telecom field."

"Did they send a picture? A link to her Facebook page perhaps?" I gave him a smirk. "She sounds hot. I don't think I've ever had a Candice."

"This isn't Match.com, for Christ sake," Henry said, giving me a look over the top of the glasses. "They don't submit photographs with the resumes."

"Pity." The ball went up and down.

He tucked the resume back into the folder, then leaned and cleared his throat. "Do me a favor, Tanner," he said with a sigh. "Keep your dick in your pants this time, will you?"

I caught the ball in my right hand while looking at him. I put on a confused face. "Henry, what are you talking about? My dick is always in my pants."

"Except when it's inside some random woman that's struck your fancy," he said, rolling his eyes. Henry had always considered himself to be like a wise uncle to me. He gave me the look you'd give a child with burnt fingers as you're explaining why they shouldn't have touched a hot stove eye.

He said, "Look, I know it's not my place to tell you what to do."

"Or who to stick my dick in," I added with a grin. I shook the ball at him. "Henry, relax. Do you need to squeeze my ball?"

"Not even remotely funny," he said, tugging off the glasses and tucking them inside his suit jacket. He blew out a long breath. "You know what I'm talking about. You can screw all the actresses and models and strippers you want, but this time, please, for me, don't screw anyone that's a part of this deal."

I had had a brief dalliance with the wife of the CEO of a company we had sought to acquire several years ago, and it caused quite a stir in the business world.

Okay, maybe "brief dalliance" is not the correct term. Her husband caught be fucking her from behind on his desk right before the papers were to be signed.

Regrettably, the deal fell through.

Henry never let me live it down.

I swung my chair around and planted my elbows on the desk. I squeezed the ball between my hands and smiled. "But Henry, if you can't screw your business associates, or their wives or daughters or girlfriends, who can you screw? I mean, what's the point of having all this money if I can't screw who I want?"

"You're worth two-billion dollars, Tanner. You can screw just about anyone you want. I'm just asking you to keep it in your pants until we're finished with this deal."

I held up three fingers in a Scout's salute. "Henry, you have my solemn pledge that I will do my best to keep my dick in my pants until this deal is done."

"Wish I could believe that," Henry said. The phone in his pocket buzzed. He pulled it out and slid open the screen. "The team from Goldman & Stern are here. They're waiting for us in the executive conference room. Come on, you need to meet them."

I made a sour face at him. The only thing I hated more than reading lengthy reports from expensive consultants was actually meeting with them.

I hated consultants.

Especially management consultants.

They were all so arrogant and smug, like they knew some horrible secret that could fuck up your business and they wouldn't share it with you until you wrote them a fat check.

They were like leeches, sucking the blood from real businesses because they weren't smart enough to start their own.

They were like the little fish that swam behind sharks so they could eat their scraps rather than fend for themselves.

They were all just so... consulting.

You get the point.

I hated fucking consultants.

And I was using fucking as an adjective, not a verb...

Hmmm... had I ever fucked a consultant? I didn't think so, but there was a first time for everything.

I leaned back in the chair and brought my bare feet up to rest on the desk. Henry winced at the dirty bottoms of my feet.

He was second in command and dressed in three-piece suits.

I was the boss and I typically came to work in ratty jeans, tennis shoes, and t-shirts.

I picked up my phone and wiggled my toes at him. "You deal with the Goldman people. I'm waiting on the call about the Ferrari."

"Tanner, they're here to meet with the both of us," he said, shoving my feet to the floor. He dusted off his hands and growled at me. "Now put on your fucking shoes and let's go. And behave yourself."

"God, you're such a kill joy," I said, looking under my desk for my tennis shoes. By the time I found my shoes and put them on, Henry was already out the door.

I picked up the stress ball and took my time catching up.

CHAPTER THREE: Candice

"Okay, let me do the talking when they get here," Stan Robbins said, lowering his voice and waving his hand at the rest of us seated at the table next to him.

Stan was in his fifties, tall and gaunt, with thinning hair and a tendency to stick his sharp nose squarely up the client's ass. Stan was the senior telecom consultant at Goldman & Stern and my immediate boss.

Juliette Ruiz, a sour-looking woman in her forties, was Stan's second in charge. Juliette, who was so thin her clothes hung off her like a hanger, hated everyone except Stan. And if she hadn't reported to Stan, she would have hated him, too. They were Goldman's power couple when it came to telecom. Together, they had over fifty years of telecom experience, and were leading the team conducting the final due diligence for Wright Enterprises' acquisition of Anderson Telecommunications.

Bob Gaines sat next to Juliette with his hands folded neatly on the table in front of him. Bob was a balding forensic accountant who had the look and pallor of a mortician. It was a fitting comparison because Bob could find financial skeletons in even the darkest of corporate closets. He not only looked like a mortician, he had the personality to match.

Between Bob and I sat Irving Hunt, Goldman's legal expert in the telecom sector. Irving was a head shorter than me and several times my age. Rumor around Goldman was that Irving could sleep with his eyes open during meetings. I kept watching him from the corner of my eye, waiting for any sign that he was nodding off.

I was there because I'd been on several telecom teams in the last year and had a good handle on the industry. My input was valuable, but I wasn't fooling myself. I was the low girl on the totem pole. I would be the one getting coffee and donuts and making copies of documents. And I would be the recipient of most of Juliette's angry stares.

That was just fine with me. A few years from now I'd be sitting in Stan's chair pulling down half a mill a year, and some other slab of fresh meat would be fetching my coffee.

A tall, distinguished-looking man with salt and pepper hair entered the room and Stan jumped up to shake his hand. I recognized him from my Google research as Henry Costas, Tanner Wright's former professor at MIT, and for the last ten years, his right-hand man at Wright Enterprises. He would be our primary point of contact for the project.

Stan introduced Costas to the team. Costas leaned across to give everyone a welcoming smile and a handshake. I noticed his eyes lingered just a bit longer on me than they did on anyone else.

I immediately wondered if I should have put my long hair up in a more business-like bun rather than letting it fall naturally around my shoulders.

God, I hated how self-conscious men could make me feel with just a casual glance.

I was dressed professionally in a dark blue suit and grey top. My big boobs were squeezed into a bra that was supposed to make them look smaller and I was barely wearing any makeup or jewelry.

Still, Costas continued to glance at me as if I were a fox trying to get into his hen house. He took the chair at the end of the table across from Stan and finally released me from his gaze.

Douchebag.

"Tanner will be right in," Costas said with a quick smile. He looked at the three of them and held out his hands. He didn't look my way again. "Would anyone like coffee or tea?"

"We're all good," Stan said, answering for the group. He glanced at the thick folder Costas had brought into the meeting with him. "I trust our proposal is in good order?"

Costas nodded as he opened the folder. "Yes, my team went through your proposal and we believe you have a good handle on everything that requires further verification at Anderson." He glanced up and smiled at Stan. "As I told you over the phone, telecom is not normally in our wheelhouse, so we're looking to you to make sure everything is good to go before we sign the final acquisition documents next week."

"No worries," Stan said, patting the air with his hands. "If anything is out of order, my team will find it."

"Very good," Costas said with a curt nod. He flipped through a few more pages and took out what looked like a contract. There were two copies. He slid one in front of Stan and kept one for himself.

"The contract is good to go," Costas said, reaching inside his suit jacket for a pen. "It's been vetted by our legal department and yours, so I'm ready to sign if you are."

"I am ready," Stan said eagerly. Stan already had the expensive Monte Blanc pen Goldman had awarded him for twenty years of service in his hand. He knew he'd be signing this contract today, so he'd probably had the pen in his hand for hours.

He twisted off the cap and with great flourish, scratched his signature on the signature line on behalf of Goldman & Stern.

Costas signed on behalf of Wright Enterprises. I noticed he was using a disposable Bic pen with the company name on the side. That said something about him to me. He was either so humble that he didn't feel the need to show off by using a thousand-dollar pen, or he was so rich that he didn't give a shit about impressing the likes of us.

My money was on the latter.

They swapped contracts and signed again.

"Very good," Stan said, taking his copy of the contract and quickly sliding it into his briefcase as if he were worried Costas might change his mind. He reached across the table and shook Costas' hand. "We'll get started first thing Monday morning."

"You must be the Goldman party," a cheery voice said from the doorway. I looked up to see Tanner Wright leaning against the doorframe with a red rubber ball in his right hand.

Unlike Henry Costas, who was impeccably dressed and perfectly put together, Tanner Wright was wearing a pair of tight jeans with the knees torn out, a pair of dingy tennis shoes, and a faded black t-shirt with the Metallica logo on the front.

He looked like someone who was there delivering pizzas rather than the billionaire entrepreneur who ran the place.

His photos on Google did not do him justice. He had a dark summer tan, even in winter. He had shaggy blonde hair that hung over his forehead. He had bright blue eyes and an easy smile that made me want to smile back, though I resisted the urge to do so.

I knew he had played soccer and rugby in college. He had maintained his physique. His round shoulders and chest pushed against the t-shirt as his waist tapered into the tight jeans. I could see lean ropes of muscle in his forearm as he squeezed the ball. I could also see a bulge in the front of the tight jeans that made the breath catch in my throat.

I swallowed hard and forced myself to look down at the table.

You couldn't tell by looking at him that he was one of the richest men on the planet. Maybe that was the point. Maybe it was a disguise. He was so rich that he tried not to look rich. It was like Brad Pitt, who did his best to look unattractive when he wasn't starring in a movie.

Jesus, nice bulge or not, he was definitely a douchebag.

Tanner tossed the ball between his hands and said, "I took as much time as I could getting here. I hope I'm too late for the meeting."

"You're not late at all," Stan said, totally missing the joke. He shot to his feet and stuck out his hand. "Stan Robbins, Mr. Wright," he said. "Goldman & Stern."

"Whoa, I don't shake hands, Stan," Tanner said quickly, taking a step back. He held up his hands as if Stan were brandishing a gun and demanding his wallet. He wrinkled his nose at Stan's hand like it was covered in dog poop.

He said, "Too many germs in the world, Stan. Plus, I have no idea where that hand has been."

Stan's hand dangled in the air for a moment, then he let it drop to his side and lowered himself into the chair. He had a look on his face like a puppy that had just been kicked by an abusive owner. Or a balloon that someone had just seen fit to pop. I almost felt sorry for him. Almost.

"We just signed the contracts, Tanner," Costas said as Tanner pulled up the chair next to him and plopped down in it. "They'll start work on Monday."

"Excellent!" Tanner said with a serious expression that was clearly for show. He blew out a long breath and squeezed the ball in his right hand as his eyes went down the table.

He briefly eyed Stan and Juliette, then Bob, then Irving. When his eyes met mine, his eyebrows slowly rose as if he had just spied an old friend. He leaned across the table and extended the hand he wouldn't let Stan shake.

He said, "You must be Candice Carlson."

I blinked at him for a moment. I glanced down the table at my compatriots. Their eyes were glued to Tanner's hand dangling in the air between us. He wiggled his fingers. I reached out to shake his hand. When our fingers touched, the pop of static electricity caused both of us to jerk our hands back.

"Whoa!" Tanner fell back in his chair with a grin on his face.

I put my hands in my lap and bit my tongue. Did he do that on purpose? Did he drag his feet across the carpet to build up static electricity in his body just so he could make me look like an idiot?

Who would do something like that?

Oh yeah, a douchebag...

"Shocking to meet you, Miss Carlson," he said with a smirk.

I forced a polite smile for the sake of the ten-million-dollar contract in Stan's briefcase.

"Yes, nice to meet you, Mr. Wright."

"Am I?" he asked.

I blinked at him. "Are you what?"

"Mister Right?"

I stared at him with my mouth hanging open, unsure what to say.

"Okay then, let's wrap this up," Costas said suddenly, clapping his hands together like he was breaking a huddle. He pushed himself up from the table and set a hand on Tanner's shoulder to keep him in the chair. It was the move of a parent trying to control an unruly toddler.

Tanner's eyes remained on mine. He gave me a little smile, like it was all a joke that only he and I were in on.

Costas directed his attention to Stan and put on a serious face. "I assume you'll be flying to Tucson on Monday to meet with Anderson's accounting team?"

"Yes, that's correct," Stan said, getting to his feet. His eyes darted between the two men across from him. Costas was looking back at him. Tanner was still looking at me. Stan turned to gesture at his team. "The four of us will be in Tucson on Monday afternoon. The itinerary was already set in anticipation of signing the contract."

"We'll meet you there," Tanner said. He was still looking at me. Still smiling. It was starting to creep me out. It was also starting to turn me on.

Was he playing some kind of weird *Fifty Shades of Grey* game with me?

Was this his idea of foreplay?

Was I supposed to rip off my clothes and lay on the table and spread my legs and beg him to fuck me?

Hmmm...

I put on a blank face as I filed that thought away for later use.

"We'll meet them there?" Costas asked, looking down at Tanner.

"We will," Tanner said, finally taking his eyes off mine and directing them toward Stan. "We have meetings scheduled with Anderson's executive team later in the week. We might as well get an early start."

He got out of the chair and gave Costas a nod.

"Call Anderson and tell them we'll all be there on Monday instead of Wednesday."

"What if they can't meet on Monday?" Costas asked. His forehead lined as he held up arm and checked his watch. "It's nearly five o'clock on Friday. That's awfully short notice."

"Then we'll have to find something to occupy our time until Wednesday, won't we," Tanner said, glancing at me yet again. Everyone turned to look at me. I felt myself literally shrinking before their eyes.

"Okay, I'll make the arrangements," Costas said, narrowing his eyes, bouncing them between Tanner and me.

Shit.

I didn't have to be a mind reader to know what Costas was thinking.

He was going to kick me off the team because Tanner was acting like a fucking teenage boy. I was the innocent bystander at this train wreck, but I would be the one held responsible for running the Tanner train off the track.

Tanner Wright's sexploits were legendary, thanks to gossip sites like TMZ and Gawker.

He had the well-earned reputation of being the billionaire bad boy who had torpedoed billion-dollar business deals because he couldn't keep his dick in his pants. And now his childish antics were about to cost me my spot on the team.

Son of a bitch.

What a DOUCHEBAG!!

Well, if they expected me to take this lying down, they were messing with the wrong girl. I set my hands on the table and laced my fingers together and stared at them.

I could feel steam coming out of my ears. Just let them try to bounce me from the team, I thought. Just let them try...

Tanner held the ball in front of him and bounced it in his palm. "In fact, there's no need for you guys to fly out commercial. We'll all take the corporate jet out together. It'll be fun."

Tanner gave everyone a quick smile, then handed the rubber ball to Costas and left the room, leaving all of us to wonder what the heck just happened.

CHAPTER FOUR: Candice

It was a quiet car ride back to our offices at Goldman & Stern because the other members of my team were as dumbfounded as I was by the actions of Tanner Wright.

The silence in the car spoke volumes.

I knew what they were all thinking. They were wondering how long it would take for Stan to boot me off the team, even though I hadn't done a thing to deserve getting the axe.

Juliette was sitting in the front passenger seat and Stan was driving. I was in the back seat, scotched between Bob and Irving. Bob stared out the window the entire way back to the office. Irving was sitting up straight with his eyes open, softly snoring.

Every now and then, I'd catch Stan glancing at me in the rear-view mirror. When our eyes met, he quickly looked away.

Juliette sat staring straight ahead and didn't say a word. I could almost hear her teeth gnashing.

I was sure Tanner's behavior in the meeting would be the talk of Goldman when we got back and Juliette got the gossip mill started. She'd like nothing better than to see me kicked off the team even though I posed no threat to her. That was just Juliette's way. She simply didn't like other women. She was more of a male chauvinist that any man I'd ever met. If she had her way, she would be the only woman working at Goldman, if not the only woman on the planet.

All I could do was shake my head and bite my tongue. I'd deal with Stan when the time came; which I knew would be soon.

Tanner Wright's smirking face flashed into my mind. I could hear the pop of electricity as our fingers touched. I could smell the faint hint of ozone in the air. He had won the Douchebag of the Century Award, hands down. I had never met anyone so cocky and full of himself.

Fine, he was a hot billionaire with a big bulge in his pants, but did he have to pull me into his silly little game?

I was completely innocent in all this. It would be remarkably unfair to kick me off the team just because of Tanner's actions.

Turned out, Stan felt otherwise. After he parked the car in the underground garage and the others were headed toward the bank of elevators, he asked me to hang back.

"What was that all about back there?" he asked with an air of accusation to his tone.

"I have no idea what that was, Stan," I said, huffing at him. "Probably just another rich asshole jerking us around. Isn't that the way this works? We're management consultants. We get jerked around by rich assholes then bill them a thousand dollars an hour for it?"

"It was more than that," Stan said, rubbing his chin as he studied me with narrow eyes. "You've never met him before, have you?"

"No, never."

"Never had any contact with him at all?"

"None."

I knew where this was going. I've never been one to bite my tongue and I was too good at my job to fear losing it, so I spread out my hands and gave it to him straight.

"Look, Stan, if you're thinking about bouncing me off this project because Tanner Wright is a flirt, you can forget it. You need me on this team. Nobody knows the digital side of telecom like I do. I'm a consummate professional and you know it."

"I know you're a professional, Candice," Stan said with a sigh. "I'm just not so sure about Tanner Wright."

* * *

I didn't even bother going up to the office. I knew Juliette was already up there telling anyone who would listen how I disrupted the meeting by flirting with Tanner Wright.

She wouldn't tell the whole story, of course.

Her version would undoubtedly have me oohing and goohing at him with my tits hanging out.

By Monday, I'd be fodder for the office gossip mill.

I'd be branded as the junior consultant who almost killed a ten-million-dollar deal because she couldn't resist flirting the bad boy billionaire.

It would all be a lie, but it wouldn't matter.

The only saving grace was that it was after five on Friday afternoon, and most of the Goldman employees would already be headed for home.

It was little solace.

I caught a cab and made it home around six. I held it together as I rode the elevator up to my tenth-floor apartment. I hurried down the hall and unlocked my door.

The moment I stepped inside and locked the door behind me, I fell to my knees and began to sob.

The hard, crusty shell that I wrapped myself in every day to face the world was left cracked and broken outside my door.

In here, all alone, it was just me, Candice Marie Carlson, the insecure farm girl from Nebraska who was doing her best to get ahead and hold it together in a cruel and unfair world.

Candice Carlson, the girl who was sitting on the floor in the dark with her back against the door to keep the world outside.

Candice Carlson, the girl who cried herself to sleep many nights because the emotional armor she wore to battle the demons of the world was so heavy that it squeezed the emotions out of her like a juice press.

Candice Carlson, the girl who was hard as stone on the outside, but soft as marshmallow on the inside.

I put my forearms on my knees and rest my head on my arms.

I sat there and cried until I had no more tears to give.

CHAPTER FIVE: Candice

It was amazing what a good cry does for the soul. It's something men will never understand. The weight of the world can be bearing down on you like a Mac truck, but sit on the floor and sob like a baby for an hour and suddenly, all is right with the world.

Or at least as right as it could get at that moment.

Throw in a microwave pizza, a pint of mint chocolate chip Haagen-Dazs, and half a bottle of chardonnay, and suddenly the world is a beautiful place.

At least the world inside my apartment.

I was more than a little drunk as I ran myself a hot bath and prepared to soak for an hour or two. As the tub filled with steaming hot water, I lit several candles and turned off the lights. The aroma of cinnamon and wildflowers wafted on the air.

I closed and locked the bathroom door. Call me weird, but I can't take a bath or a shower with the door open. Guess I've seen too many movies about silly girls who take showers when murderers were lurking around.

I know, I'm a psychiatrist's wet dream. Oh well.

I set my iPhone on the counter and told Siri to play some Van Morrison to set the mood. I stripped off the sweats that I'd changed into after my crying jag in the foyer, and stood naked in front of the mirror to put up my hair.

As I bundled my long hair into a bun and pinned it to the top of my head, I let my eyes take stock of the woman in the mirror. It was something that I did at the end of every day.

Did the day add a new line or wrinkle?

Are my boobs sagging?

Do I have stretch marks on my stomach?

Again, a psychiatrist would have a field day with me.

I was tall for a girl at five-eight, and curvy for my height.

I inherited my mom's big boobs and round hips. My boobs hung off my chest like two large melons that had never been squeezed. My areolas contrasted darkly against the milky whiteness of my breasts. I kept my blond pubes trimmed short.

I took a deep breath as I brought my hands down from my hair to cup my breasts. I brushed a finger over my nipples and they responded immediately, growing hard at my touch.

I closed my eyes. Suddenly, in my mind, Tanner Wright was standing behind me with his hands resting softly on my hips. His sudden appearance startled me for a moment, but my mind told me to just relax and let the fantasy flow.

I could feel Tanner's fingers digging gently into my hips. I felt his thumbs at the small of my back, gently massaging the dimples above my ass.

I rolled my head to the side and moaned as he pressed his lips to my shoulder. He nibbled his way up my neck and to my ear. He took my earlobe between his teeth and bit down just enough to hurt in the most wonderful way.

I could feel his hot breath in my ear.

His tongue followed his breath.

He licked the rim of my ear and darted his tongue inside. A shudder went through me as I could feel the hot juices pooling between my legs.

Tanner's hands came around to cup my tits. He squeezed the nipples between his fingers. He moaned in my ear.

I felt his cock pressing into my back; long, hard, wet from his juices. He slid his cock up and down my back. I could feel his balls rubbing against my ass.

I braced my hands on the sink and wiggled my ass into him. He slid his cock up and down through the crack in my ass. His hands slid down from my breasts and met at my clit. He rolled my clit between his thumbs. I could feel the orgasm building from deep within my body, like a match that would soon start a raging fire.

Tanner continued sliding his cock against me as his hands worked my pussy. He slid his fingers across my folds to lubricate them, then teased my opening.

"Fuck me, Tanner," I heard myself moan. "Take my cherry. Make it yours forever."

I pushed my ass toward him and leaned the top half of my body forward, offering my pussy to him. I felt his hands on my hips again as he positioned himself behind me. I felt the head of his cock pressing into my hole. I held my breath in anticipation. He slid in just the head and paused for a moment. I felt my pussy spreading to accommodate him.

There was no virgin pain as he dug his fingers into my hips and slid himself fully inside of me. I stood on my tiptoes to give him the perfect angle. He started sliding his cock in and out, in and out. My big boobs swayed beneath me with every thrust.

"Oh... my... god..."

My words were carried on gusts of hot breath.

"Faster... harder... more..."

Tanner was hammering into me now. My tits swayed. I moaned and called his name as the orgasm hit.

"I'm... cumming... oh... my... god..."

I squeezed my eyes tightly together and sucked in a long breath as I came. Tanner's cock plunged in and out of me until I begged him to stop. I felt his touch drift away from my body like a warm passing wind.

I opened my eyes and looked in the mirror, which was fogged up from the steaming water that was about to overflow the tub.

I blinked back to reality and gazed down at myself.

My left hand was clutching my breast. My breast was red from the hard rubbing and squeezing. My nipple stood on end, a dark crimson thimble in a sea of white.

I was standing with my knees bent.

The fingers of my right hand were buried inside my cunt.

My hand was drenched to the wrist from the orgasm I'd given myself.

I let my fingers slide out of me and braced my palms on the counter.

I took in a long, deep breath, then let it out slowly.

It all seemed so real that I turned to look around the bathroom, as if I'd find Tanner standing there.

Sadly, I was alone.

I turned off the water and lowered myself into the steaming tub.

I closed my eyes and smiled as the hot water engulfed me.

I picked up the bar of soap from the edge of the tub and rubbed it between my legs as the fantasy began to replay in my mind.

This time I was a spectator rather than a participant.

You know how they say that if you lose the use of one of your senses, it makes the other senses heighten?

Like, if you lose your sense of sight, your senses of smell and hearing and taste and touch grow stronger?

The same was true when you were a virgin.

When you'd never had a real man inside you, your imagination intensified until it became as vivid as the real thing.

Thank God.

Sigh...

CHAPTER SIX: Tanner

Monday morning, 7:45 AM.

I noted the time because Henry was supposed to pick me up for our trip to Tucson with the Goldman team around eight-thirty. I had my assistant pack a bag over the weekend and it was sitting next to the front door, ready to go.

That was my motto: always be prepared.

Or have an assistant prepare it for you.

I had time to kill, so I fixed a cup of coffee using the twenty-thousand-dollar brewing machine Henry had convinced me to buy during a business trip to Italy a few years back.

It was supposedly the best coffee brewing system on the planet. The coffee beans the system also supposedly brewed the best cup of coffee on the planet. I think the beans were imported from the deepest jungles of Columbia and had been shit through a tiger's ass or some such nonsense.

I didn't get the big deal. The coffee it brewed was mediocre at best. It had the consistency and the smell of burnt ink. It certainly was not a twenty-thousand-dollar cup of coffee. The hundred dollar Keurig in my office made better coffee.

Henry said I had the palette of a caveman.

What-the-fuck-ever, dude.

I knew a shitty cup of coffee when I tasted it.

I kept meaning to buy a Starbucks franchise and install it downstairs off the lobby (I own this building and live in the penthouse), but I kept forgetting to call Starbucks CEO Howard Schulz to make the deal.

I picked up my iPhone and spoke into it.

"Siri, remind me to put a Starbucks in the lobby downstairs."

Siri confirmed my brilliance and I set the phone aside.

I set the mug of steaming coffee on the kitchen table and fired up my laptop. I logged into Facebook and tapped my fingers on the keys.

I ignored the 1,835 notifications and 2,018 messages that flashed at the top of the screen.

The truth is, I hate fucking Facebook and only use it to dig up dirt about people I might be doing business with.

Or people that simply fascinated me.

People like Candice Carlson.

I was constantly amazed at some of the things people posted on Facebook. They just put it out there for all the world to see, without any concern of consequences.

Hey look, here's a shot of you getting shit-faced drunk at a bachelor party.

Hey look, here's a shot of you in the bathroom with a naked hooker from the party.

Hey look, here's you getting a lap dance from said hooker.

Oh look, look, look! Here's a picture of you doing a line of some white powder that looks an awful lot like coke off the hooker's tit!

Ah, finally, the coup de grace... here's a picture of you passed out drunk in the hotel room naked and covered in magic marker.

Oh look, someone drew a happy face on the head of your dick.

I had found all those wonderful images when digging into the background of a guy who wanted to be my Chief Financial Officer at a salary of four-hundred-grand a year.

I just went to his Facebook page, hit Photos, and bam!

I took great joy in showing him what I had found, then asking, "So, you want me to let you manage my company's financials? Seriously? Uh, I don't think so. Thank you, drive through."

Okay, granted, I put the poor guy through hours and hours of grueling interviews before I sprang the Facebook pics and told him to fuck off. But hey, a guy's gotta have a little fun. Right?

I typed in Candice Carlson's name into the search bar and sipped the shitty coffee as I waited for her profile to pop up. I wondered what embarrassing moments or tantalizing tidbits I would find on her page.

And like magic, there was Candice Carlson's life in full living color for all the world to see.

"Okay, Candice Carlson," I said with a grin. "Let's see what deep dark secrets I can surmise from your lovely profile."

I clicked to enlarge her profile picture and was disappointed to find that it was a standard bullshit company portrait, probably the pulled from her bio on the Goldman website.

"Shit," I said as I clicked to close the enlarged image. "Come on, Candice. Don't let me down."

I went back to her profile page and clicked on the "About Candice" link. Standard stuff: twenty-five, Harvard MBA grad, hometown Ottumwa, Nebraska, population who gives a shit.

"Single is good," I said, noting her relationship status.

I clicked on her Photos, hoping to find a drunk party pic or two or three. Or Candice at the beach in a string bikini with her tits hanging out.

Woo-hoo! Wouldn't that be a fucking awesome way to start the day! A hot bikini shot of Candice that I could rub one out to before leaving the penthouse.

"Shit," I said again as her photos loaded on the screen. "So much for whacking off to Candice's tits."

There's Candice at a business event.

There's Candice at a fundraiser.

There's Candice at a formal dinner.

There's Candice with a group of sorority sisters.

There's Candice in her cap and gown.

"Son of a bitch," I said with a sigh. I pushed the computer away in disgust and picked up the coffee cup. "Are you really that fucking boring, Candice Carlson? You couldn't give me one decent tit pick to start my day?"

My iPhone buzzed with a text message from Henry. He was downstairs with the car. Crap. My quest to learn more about Candice Carlson would have to wait.

I stared at her utterly boring profile picture for a moment.

I closed the laptop and shook my head.

Candice Carlson needed a little excitement in her life.

And fortunately for her, I was just the guy to give it to her.

CHAPTER SEVEN: Tanner

I handed the driver my suitcase so he could stow it in the trunk, then climbed into the back of the limo to sit next to Henry, who grunted at me and continued fiddling with his phone.

"Bad manners to use your phone at the table, my son," I said, shaking my head at him.

"Sorry, just shooting an email off to Stan Roberts at Goldman confirming our flight time for today." He tucked the phone inside his Armani jacket and directed his full attention to me.

"So, how was your weekend?" he asked.

"Fine," I said with a shrug. "I didn't do much. Just flew out to Vegas to look at the Ferrari I bought."

"Did you drive it back?"

I snorted at him. "You don't actually drive a car like that Henry. I had them load it onto a climate-controlled car hauler I borrowed from Earnhardt for transport back to Chicago. It should arrive in a day or two."

A look of judgment came to his eye. "How much did you end up spending? On a car?"

I waved a hand at him, as if the question smelled bad, but not as bad as my answer. "I spent more than I should have, but not as much as I would have."

"Tanner, how much?"

I blew out a long sigh. "Twenty-eight-point-seven mill for the car and another ten-percent in auction fees," I said, shrugging off the number like it was pocket change, because that's what it was to me. He scowled at me. "Okay, so it went a little over estimate. It's not a big deal. In five years, it will double in value."

"I hope you're right," he said, shaking his head.

"I'm always right."

"Are you?"

I glanced over to see him scowling at me. I held out my hands and asked, "What's up your ass this morning?"

"Your little show on Friday with the Goldman people is what's up my ass," Henry said. He gave me the look my dad used to give me whenever I disappointed him, which was most of the time. He shook his head slowly and clicked his tongue. "I'm not going to let you blow this deal, Tanner. It's too important."

"I'm not going to blow the deal, Henry," I said, giving him a dismissive wave. "I really don't understand why you're so upset. I thought I was quite the gentleman in that meeting."

"Of course, you were."

He blew out a long breath and shook his head again. Some days Henry shook his head so much that I expected it to come loose from his neck.

He said, "Do you have any idea the position you have put me in with the Goldman people? And with Anderson, asking them to completely rework their executive team's schedule for the week?"

I huffed. "I don't give a shit about the Goldman people. They work for us, remember? And the Anderson executive team will be out on their ears the moment the final documents are signed if they're not careful."

"Well, I do give a shit about them," Henry said seriously. "Unlike you, I don't have billions of dollars that lead me to think that I can be a total ass in front of people. Honestly, Tanner, sometimes you act like a spoiled teenager rather than a successful business man. What is your deal?"

"I don't have a deal," I said with a sigh. "I just get bored and I like fucking with people. I keep telling you to stop making me attend meetings, but you keep insisting on bringing me along."

"Because, like it or not, you are the face of Wright Enterprises. You're the bad boy that gets all the press. You're the guy that does the

Ted Talks that make millennials hang on your every word and spend millions on your products."

"Do they really?" I asked, pretending to be serious. "Hang on my every word?"

Henry threw up his hands. "You're being ridiculous."

I patted his knee. "Henry, you have my word that I will not do anything to mess up this deal. Scouts honor. Cross my heart and hope to die."

"You were never a scout," Henry said, glancing out the window as if he could no longer stand to look at me. "And honor is something you know nothing about."

"Ouch," I said with a smile.

Still facing the window, he said, "I emailed Stan Roberts and told him to leave Candice Carlson in Chicago."

My eyebrows shot up. "You what?"

He turned to stare me down. I had never seen Henry look more serious. "I told Stan that Candice can remain on the team, but it would be best if she operates from their office in Chicago. So, she will not be coming to Tucson with us."

Now it was my turn to be sanctimonious.

I asked, "Do you think that's really fair to Miss Carlson? The poor girl did nothing but show up to a meeting. If anyone should be knocked out of going to Tucson, it's me, not her."

"Fairness has nothing to do with it," he said. "And you have to go. There is no getting out of it."

"Then what's the problem?"

"The problem is that she was a distraction to you in the meeting. Therefore, I expect that she would be a distraction to you in Tucson. And we can't have you distracted."

I shook my head and gave him the disappointed look he so often gave me. "Henry, I thought you were smarter than that."

He frowned. "What does that mean?"

I tapped a finger to my chin and made a thoughtful face.

"Would you rather have me distracted and out of the way in Tucson? Or would you rather have me attend all the big meetings and do everything I could to kill the deal?"

Henry's mouth dropped open as the little lights came on inside his perfectly-coiffed head. He tugged his iPhone from his jacket and found Stan Roberts direct cell number.

"Stan, Henry Costas," he said, smiling at me. "Please disregard the email I sent you earlier about leaving Candice Carlson in Chicago. After further consideration, I think she will play a vital role in the success of the Anderson acquisition. Yes, that's correct. Fine. We'll see you at the airport in an hour."

CHAPTER EIGHT: Candice

The moment I arrived at Goldman on Monday morning, I received a text from Stan to come to his office. I just blew out a long breath and reconciled myself to the fact that I was being booted off the team.

I had cried myself dry over the weekend, so this morning there were no more tears to give. I put on my armor and emerged from my apartment ready to do battle and take whatever hits the day might bring.

Candice Carlson, the girl who wore her heart on her sleeve and cried at the drop of a dime, was left at the apartment.

Candice Carlson, corporate cunt and hard-assed bitch emerged.

In a moment of pure optimism, I had packed a suitcase for the trip and brought it to the office. I dropped it off in my office on the way to see Stan. There was no way I was going to show up at his door with a suitcase and the assumption that everything was just peachy. Everything wasn't peachy. I could feel it in my bones.

Stan was standing behind his desk neatly stacking papers into his briefcase when I tapped on his door. Juliette, Bob, and Irving were sitting on the couch in Stan's office like the three monkeys that see, hear, and speak no evil. Bob and Irving stared into their coffee cups. Juliette had her eyes glued on Bob. There was a slight smirk of satisfaction on her face.

"Morning, Stan," I said, forcing a smile to keep the tears at bay.

"Morning," Stan said curtly, glancing up at me. He stared into my eyes for a moment, no doubt choosing the words that would let me down the quickest and easiest. I was dumbfounded when the corners of his lips curled into a smile.

"Just wanted to get everyone together to let you know what the itinerary is for the week," he said. He came around the desk with four pieces of paper and handed them out to the group.

"Henry Costas emailed that to me earlier. I forwarded a copy of the email to each of you, but I wanted to give you a hard copy we can review in the car on the way to the airport."

"That's it?" Juliette asked. She cut her eyes at me. They all did. They all seemed a little surprised that I was still on the team. I certainly was.

"That's it," Stan said, moving back around the desk to finish packing his briefcase. He held up his wristwatch when nobody moved. "That's it. Let's go, people. The car leaves for the airport in twenty minutes. I'll meet you all downstairs."

* * *

The Wright Enterprises corporate jet was fueled and ready for takeoff when we arrived at the private hangar. We were met by Henry Costas on the tarmac, but I didn't see Tanner anywhere.

That was probably a good thing. After the hot imaginary sex we'd had, I wasn't sure if I could keep from blushing when we came face to face.

The Wright corporate jet was as over the top and impressive as its owner. Pristine white on the outside with the bright red Wright Enterprises logo on the tail; expensive leathers and exotic woods on the inside.

There were eight passenger seats, four on each side of the plane. The seats were configured in sets of two that faced inward to a small table between them.

I buckled in across from Bob for the three-hour trip to Tucson. Henry Costas sat across from Stan. Juliette took the seat directly behind Stan and spent most of the trip hovering over them like an over-eager stewardess. Irving put on a pair of dark sunglasses and would probably sleep the entire way.

After the fastest and smoothest take-off I've ever experienced (it was literally like being inside a bullet fired into the air), I opened my laptop to review the itinerary for the week. I looked around the cabin.

Still no sign of Tanner. I wondered if he'd changed his mind about joining us in Tucson.

A few minutes into the flight, a man's deep voice crackled over the speakers mounted in the ceiling above our heads. "Ladies and gentleman, welcome to Wright Enterprises flight number 69 with nonstop service from Chicago, Illinois to Tucson, Arizona."

I smiled. There was something vaguely familiar about the pilot's voice.

"There are blue skies ahead and we should arrive in Tucson in approximately three hours, twelve minutes, and sixty-nine seconds."

Bob frowned at me and pointed at the speaker above his head. "Is that Tanner Wright's voice?"

"The aircraft we are flying today is a brand-spanking new Gulfstream G650 with a price tag of seventy-two-million dollars and sixty-nine cents. The Gulfstream G650 will comfortably accommodate eight passengers and four crew members, can travel up to 7,000 nautical miles nonstop at a max speed of 0.925 Mach, making it the fastest private jet money can buy. I mean, that's really fucking fast, people."

I rolled my eyes at Bob. "Yep. The great one himself."

"So, ladies and gents, on behalf of the real captain and your flight crew, I hope you enjoy your flight and if there's anything you need, please don't hesitate to ask." The speaker was silent for a moment, then he added, "Oh, over and under, I mean over and over, I mean, ah fuck it, you know what I mean."

I did my best to appear unimpressed, but I was grinning like the Cheshire Cat on the inside. Tanner may have been an obnoxious douchebag billionaire, but he was growing on me. Just a little.

A moment later, the cockpit door sprang open and Tanner appeared with a satisfied grin on his face. He was wearing his usual jeans and a t-shirt, but had added a black sports jacket and a pilot's cap. He was still wearing the ratty tennis shoes and no socks.

He came through the cabin like a whirlwind, greeting everyone, asking if he could take our drink orders, asking is we needed our membership card to the mile-high club validated. When his little show was over, he set the pilot's cap on Bob's head and asked if he might borrow his seat.

Bob was as thick as mud when it came to taking subtle hints. He adjusted the cap on his bald head to ride low over his eyes, but didn't take it off. He peered up at Tanner with a look of confusion on his face. "I'm sorry, you want to borrow my seat?"

"If you don't mind, Captain sir," Tanner said, snapping a salute and clicking his heels together. "There's another seat over there across from the gentleman who appears to be dead or sleeping very soundly."

Bob craned his head to look at Irving, then looked up at Tanner and forced a smile. "Sure, I mean, all the seats are the same. Right?"

"That they are," Tanner said, taking Bob's hand and tugging him out of the seat. He patted Bob on the back and pointed at the seat across from Irving. "So, since they're all the same, you won't mind taking that one."

I watched as Tanner made a show of escorting Bob to the other seat. He called over one of the flight attendants who stood like sentinels at the back of the plane and asked her to please take good care of his best pal, Bob.

The flight attendant, a gorgeous redhead that looked as if she'd just fallen out of a magazine, put a hand on Bob's shoulder and promised to take good care of him. Bob gazed up at her like a pound puppy falling in love with its new owner.

I glanced around the cabin. All eyes were on me. Costas and Stan sported matching frowns. If Juliette's eyes were lasers, they would have already burned through my head.

Fuck them, I thought.

I have not done anything wrong or inappropriate. I am not going to let these people diminish my worth.

I am not going to let them judge me.

I am not going to run into the bathroom and cry like a baby.

I am not going to cry.

I am not.

I am...

"Wow, I didn't think he would ever leave," Tanner said with a broad grin as he slid into the seat across from me. He signaled the other flight attendant and she immediately appeared at our table.

"Well, hello, Patricia," Tanner said with a playful look. "How are you today?"

Patricia, who was the blond clone of the redhead, put her hands behind her back and gave him a picture-perfect smile. "I'm excellent today, Mr. Wright. How are you?"

"You certainly are," he said, smiling up at her. "And I am fine, thank you for asking."

"Can I bring you anything?" she asked.

"Yes. I would like a cup of black coffee and a honey bun."

"Yes, sir," she said. She smiled down at me. "And for you, Miss?"

I stared up at her with my mouth hanging open. She was gorgeous, but there was no pretense or condescension in her eyes. She was there but to serve at the master's whim. Lucky her.

I finally said, "Um, that sounds fine. I'll have the same."

"Don't forget to warm those buns, honey," Tanner added with a wink. I saw her smile back at him and immediately suspected there was something more between them. I mean, he was a hot billionaire playboy and she looked like a Victoria's Secret model moonlighting as a flight attendant. Who could blame either of them if they had mutually joined the mile-high club. I wondered how many times Tanner's membership card to the club had been stamped.

"So, Miss Carlson," he said with a sigh. "How was your weekend?" He leaned back in the seat and dug into his pants pocket. His fingers emerged wrapped around the red rubber ball.

"Um, it was fine, Mr. Wright. Thanks for asking."

"Look, if we're going to be working together you have to stop calling me Mr. Wright," he said, making a goofy face. "That sort of title puts a lot of pressure on a guy. Call me Tanner."

He made me smile, which made him smile.

"Okay, Tanner. Please call me Candice."

As if on cue, both of us glanced over to find the other passengers staring at us, as if we were performers on a stage and they were the dumbfounded audience witnessing a show they never expected to see. Tanner gave them a hard look and their stares quickly went away.

The attendant delivered our coffee and honey buns. I closed the laptop and stowed it under the seat to make room.

The coffee was steaming hot. I had to let it cool before attempting a sip. How awful would that be, sitting across from a handsome billionaire full of himself and innuendo, then I burn my tongue on hot coffee.

No thank you, that's one embarrassing moment I don't need.

Tanner, on the other hand, seemed to have no fear at all of scalding his tongue. He picked up the coffee and blew a cooling breath into the cup, then took a cautious slurp.

"Wow, hot," he said, smacking his lips. He set down the cup and picked up the honey bun with his free hand and bit off a huge chunk. He closed his eyes and moaned at the taste.

"Have the hot honey buns, people," he said loudly.

I watched him for a moment. He was almost like a kid; a big, rich, obnoxious kid. He was hot as hell and manly to the max, but there was an innocence there, as well. Maybe he was like me. Maybe the public Tanner and the private Tanner were two very different people. I'd probably never find out, but it certainly was an intriguing prospect.

"So, Candice, let's talk business," he said, his tone and expression turning formal again. He sucked the icing from his fingers, then wiped his hand and lips on a napkin.

He said, "Give me your thoughts on the Anderson acquisition."

"My thoughts?"

"Yes, your thoughts." He leaned in and peered at me from under his eyebrows. "You've read the acquisition documents, I assume."

I nodded. "I have."

"And you're read the company prospectus?"

"I have."

"And you have our in-house research on Anderson's financials."

"I do." I had to smile at him or my face would crack.

He held up the rubber ball between us on the tips of his fingers and fixed his eyes on it, as if it were a crystal ball that foretold the future.

"So, what do you think? Are we getting a good deal? A fair deal? Are we raping and pillaging their village? Or are we being taken to the bank? What are your thoughts?"

I licked my lips nervously. I knew everyone was listening. Stan would have told me to tell Tanner what he wanted to hear. Juliette would have told me to refer the question to Stan. But I wasn't being paid to be a yes-woman or to dodge important questions.

I cleared my throat and told him what I really thought.

"Well... Tanner, I think the price you've offered is fair, but I do have some concerns about Anderson's profit and loss statements for the last ten years. There were some discrepancies in the P&Ls that—"

Henry Costas cut me off. "Those P&L's have been fully vetted by our in-house accountants. There's no need for you to waste time there, Miss Carlson."

That was news to me. Reviewing the annual P&L's since the company opened in 1974 was one of the tasks I'd been assigned, and I told him so.

"That must have been assigned to the task list before the work was done in-house," Costas said. He looked at Stan. "Isn't that correct, Stan?"

Stan fidgeted in his seat for a moment. He didn't have a clue if that was right or not. He hemmed and hawed for a moment, then did what he always did. He said what the customer wanted to hear.

"Yes, I'm sorry, Candice, Mr. Costas is correct. You must not have the most recent task order list. I'll get that to you as soon as we land."

The latest task order list? What the heck was he talking about? I had the only task order list that had been assigned; the same task order list as the rest of the team.

I had spent most of the weekend (when I wasn't sobbing like a baby and stuffing ice cream into my face) studying four decades' worth of Anderson P&L's so I would have a jump on things in case I didn't get booted from the team.

And unless the financials that I'd been sent were wrong, as well, then there were red flags that needed to be addressed.

Tanner seemed to study Costas and Henry for a moment before turning back to me. His forearm muscles flexed as he squeezed the rubber ball. He spoke to me with his eyes. His gaze told me we'd address the red flags on Anderson's P&L later.

"Other than that, give me your thoughts on the acquisition."

Before I could answer he swept a hand at the others, who were watching and listening while trying to pretend that they weren't.

"Listen up, people, because I'm going to ask each of you the same question later."

I cleared my throat and folded my hands on the table and leaned on my elbows. "I believe the acquisition is smart, given the share price you're paying, which is $31 a share. That's $2 over market, but anything up to $40 a share would be a bargain given the value of the contracts and assets that Anderson holds."

"What about their infrastructure and expansion plans?" he asked. "According to your resume you are one of Goldman's experts on digital networks and optical fiber."

I tried to keep the smug look off my face. I wondered if anyone else on the team had even bothered to read my resume. "Their infrastructure is sound, but aging rapidly. They have contracts in place to install fiber optic networks for a number of small and medium municipalities, but the competition to move into major markets like New York, Chicago, and Atlanta, is fierce. Until those systems are in place, their customers are at the mercy of the older wired networks, which could be a concern down the road."

He narrowed his eyes at me. They all did. He knew exactly what I was talking about.

He said, "And if their old customers are at the mercy of their old technology, those customers might be attracted to a different carrier with new technology like fiber optics that offers greater connectivity and faster speeds."

"Exactly," I said, nodding. "It's not a tremendous concern now, but if companies like Charter and Spectrum install fiber optic networks faster than Anderson, well..."

"They could lure away Anderson's customers, making the company less valuable than it is today." He gave me a smile that was not filled with tricks or treats. It was one of admiration.

"Very impressive, Miss Carlson," he said.

"Candice," I shot back.

"Right. Candice."

He swiveled his chair to face the others and bounced the rubber ball on the floor between his feet. "All right then. Let's hear what the rest of you have to say."

I ate the entire honey bun and drank the coffee as I listened to the older, wiser, more-expert members of the team say basically the same things I just did.

Occasionally, Tanner would glance over and smile, as if saying, "You nailed it, girl."

I found that I couldn't keep my eyes from drifting over his body as he conducted the meeting.

Such boyish charm in a such a seriously hot and seriously brilliant package.

Maybe Tanner Wright wasn't such a douchebag after all.

CHAPTER NINE: Tanner

By the time the corporate jet touched down in Tucson, I was certain of three things.

Thing Number One: Henry was wise to hire the Goldman & Stern team to do the final due diligence on the Anderson deal. They were all very sharp and knew the industry well. I was impressed, even though I had to pull Stan's sharp nose out of my ass a time or two.

Even the angry little woman who looked like she could chew nails, the goofy accountant enamored of the pilot's cap, and the legal eagle who I think was asleep with his eyes open most of the time, all had good insight and input into the deal.

Thing Number Two: There were red flags in the Anderson P&L's that clearly Henry didn't want to discuss in front of the Goldman group. Fine, we'd address those red flags when we were alone.

Sometimes our deals required that we do things, say things, or ignore things in order to keep certain facts and figures out of the public eye. I got the feeling that Stan was caught with his pants down because he underestimated the abilities of their junior consultant.

And finally, Thing Number Three that I was certain of by the time the jet landed in Tucson was that I wanted to get to know Candice Carlson better. Much better. A lot better.

I wasn't sure exactly what was drawing me to her, but I felt like a moth being lured to a flame. I just didn't want to get my wings – or other body parts—singed.

Perhaps it was that she was beautiful in an unassuming way. You didn't have to sandblast the makeup from her face or peel back the layers of her multiple personalities to find the real woman underneath.

She was genuine, sincere, and so unlike the other women I typically spent time with.

She was intelligent, funny, warm, and down to earth. I loved the way her nose crinkled when she laughed at my stupid jokes and how the corners of her lips curled into a smile.

There was no pretense in her eyes. What you saw was what you got. I immediately loved that about her.

Candice Carlson was the real deal.

The genuine article.

The only question was: how do I get someone like her to like someone like me? It was a question asked over the ages by teenage boys, star-crossed lovers, and love struck billionaires used to getting whatever they wanted.

I knew bragging about my cars and jets and money wasn't going to impress her. No, a woman like Candice Carlson didn't care about those sorts of things.

I had a winning personality. I was funny and charming and good looking and in great shape. Oh, and modest. I was very modest. And according to dozens of women in the greater Chicago area—and around the world—one hell of a great lay.

I could impress her with the size of my dick and my ability to rock and roll all night long, but that was a Phase Two move.

I had to get her to Phase One first.

I had to get her to like me.

Then everything else would fall into place.

CHAPTER TEN: Candice

A team from Anderson Telecommunications was waiting on the tarmac when we touched down in Tucson. Tanner and Costas climbed into the back of a stretch limo with the Anderson execs and went one way, and the Goldman team was shuffled into a van driven by an assistant and ferried to the Anderson offices in downtown Tucson.

Even though the rest of the country was frozen solid, winter in Tucson felt like spring back in Nebraska. It was nearly seventy-degrees and sunny as we stepped off the plane. We all peeled off our Chicago-winter coats and left them on the plane before getting into the van.

I spent the entire day locked in a room with half a dozen analysts and a manager from Anderson's network expansion group. The task was to conduct cost analysis on their major market expansion plans. It was my job to determine if Anderson's plans were realistic or inflated to drive the acquisition stock price higher.

Stan appeared at the door around six and said to call it a day. I was never so happy to see him in my life. By the time I got settled into my hotel room, it was nearly eight o'clock and my brain was fried.

I stripped off my clothes and hung them neatly on hangers, then went in to take a quick shower. The hot water felt wonderful as it melted away the tension from my neck and shoulders.

I didn't realize how stressful the day had been, or how my muscles had tied into knots. I closed my eyes and wished that Tanner was there in the shower behind me, rubbing away the tension from my shoulders as his cock slid into me from behind.

My stomach growling forced me back to reality. I remembered that I hadn't eaten anything since the honey bun earlier in the day.

Oh well, save that fantasy for another day.

I turned off the shower and reached for a towel.

I pulled on a pair of boxer shorts and a ratty Harvard t-shirt. Some women slept in nightgowns, some in negligees, some in the nude. I dressed comfortably for bed. I had no one to impress.

I pulled my hair into a ponytail and picked up the room service menu from the dresser. I called down and ordered a cheeseburger and fries and a chocolate shake. When I was out of town, my usual healthy-eating regiment went out the window.

I picked up the remote and settled back on the bed to watch a little television until my not-so-healthy dinner arrived.

* * *

I was thirty minutes into a rerun of *The Housewives of Orange County* when someone knocked on the door. They called out, "Room service!"

"Just a minute," I called back. I clicked off the TV and hopped off the bed. I scooped my purse off the dresser so I could give the guy a tip.

When I opened the door, there stood Tanner Wright, wearing a chef's hat and pushing a cart that held an assortment of covered dishes.

"What the heck?" I asked with a wide smile. "What are you doing?"

"Delivering your dinner, madam," he said, sweeping his arms over the cart of food as if he had made it magically appear. "May I come in or would you prefer to dine in the hallway?"

I stepped aside to let him push the cart into the room. He directed me to sit on the foot of the bed and made a show of taking the covers off the dishes.

"For Madam Carlson this evening we have a lovely fresh garden salad, which, if I may recommend, you just toss in the trash because it's really just rabbit food."

He lifted the silver cover off the first plate.

"As the main course, we have a magnificent filet mignon, garnished with baby carrots and garlic mashed potatoes."

He lifted the next cover.

"For dessert, we have a lovely slice of strawberry cheese cake and to drink, we have coffee, tea, or..."

He reached beneath the cart and brought out two six packs of beer. "Coors in the bottle, my personal favorite."

"You're really something," I said with a grin. I lifted my chin and let my eyes go around the plates. "It looks like you brought enough for two."

He mocked a look of surprise. "Did I? Oh my, the kitchen must have messed up your order. I'll have them flogged at once."

"I can't eat all of that," I said with a shrug. I arched my eyebrows and smiled up at him. "Maybe you'd like to join me?"

Tanner grinned and plucked the chef's hat off his head. He tossed the chef's hat on the cart and rubbed his hands together and smiled.

"I was hoping you'd say that," he growled. "I'm famished!"

* * *

Tanner spread the food out on the little table in front of the window and we sat on opposites sides and dug in. We both ate like starving souls. The food was amazing.

We trashed the salads.

The filet melted in my mouth.

The dessert literally made me moan.

For hours, we chatted like old friends as we stuffed our bellies with food and washed it down with cold beer. Tanner talked about his life, how he started the company in his parents' garage when he was just a teenager, how he met Henry Costas at MIT and convinced him to become his partner, how he and Henry had built the company from the ground up.

There lots of victories, but I could sense a sadness when he talked about his personal life. He'd never been married. He had never even come close. He admitted to being a playboy, but in a moment of reflection, he said he would love to meet the right girl someday and start a family. I watched his eyes as he spoke. The douchebag I'd met the day before was no longer there.

He had been replaced by – dare I say – a nice guy.

Tanner leaned back with his fifth or six beer and sighed. "Yes, sir, it's been an interesting ride." He took a sip and flexed his eyebrows at me. "What about you, Candice Carlson, with your snappy business suits and an MBA from Harvard. Why is there no significant other in your life?"

I held the bottle to my lips and tried to be coy. "Who said there wasn't a significant other in my life."

"Facebooks says," he shot back.

The bottle froze at my bottom lip. "Oh, my god. You scoped me out on Facebook?"

He huffed at me. "OMG, you scoped me out on Facebook? Of course, I did. Don't you know, Facebook reveals all. And according to your relationship status, you are single."

"Why isn't there a relationship status that says none of your fucking business?"

"I think there is, actually," he said with a thoughtful pout. "It's the one right under 'fuck off and die.'"

I drained the bottle and he handed me another. Then I made the mistake of telling him about Scott, and how his mother had forced him to break up with me.

"What a pussy," he growled.

"Oh, you have no idea," I said, smacking my lips. "Scott took the word pussy to new heights."

"He set the pussy bar higher for all mankind," Tanner said seriously. "Fucking mama's boy."

"You got that right."

"Let me tell you something," he said, bobbing in and out, slurring his words a little. "If you were my girl and my mom said to dump you?"

He poked out his bottom lip and shook his head. "I'd say mom, no fucking way. Do you know how hard it is to find a nice girl out there!"

I almost blew beer though my nose. I grabbed a napkin and wiped my mouth as he grinned at my reaction. I waved my hands in front of my face to fan away the tears of laughter.

Almost in jest (almost) I asked, "So, you think I'm a nice girl?"

Tanner licked the beer from his lips and gazed into my eyes. "I think you are a very nice girl," he said. "Do you think I'm a nice boy?"

"Oh no," I said, feeling the flush of the alcohol flowing through my veins. I leaned in and batted my eyes at him. "I think you're a bad boy, Mr. Wright. A very bad boy, indeed."

I drained the bottle and slammed it on the table.

CHAPTER ELEVEN: Tanner

I gotta admit, I was a little shocked—and more than a little turned on—when Candice guzzled the remaining beer out of the bottle like a biker at a drinking contest and slammed it on the table.

She ran her tongue around her lips and blinked at me. She was a little drunk. We both were. But not so drunk that we didn't know what was about to happen.

She burped and gave me a silly smile.

I burped louder and gave her a bigger smile.

I reached across the table for her. She put her hand in mine. She got out of her chair and came around to me. She straddled my legs to sit on my thighs, and put her hands on my cheeks.

She brought her mouth to mine and stared into my eyes as her tongue darted across my lips. Then she closed her eyes and pressed her lips to mine and our tongues began to rock and roll.

In an instant, my hands were exploring her body. She was wearing a pair of loose boxer shorts. I slid my hands into the leg holes and dug my fingers into her ass cheeks. I could feel her big tits pressing into my chest. She writhed against me as we kissed. I felt my blood beginning to boil.

"No one can know," she said, breathing into my ear as I nibbled the ridge of her jaw. She had her hands on the sides of my head. She pulled my head back to look at me. "Tanner, do you hear me? No one can know."

"I hear you," I said, gazing into her eyes. "No one can know."

She stared deeply into my eyes for a moment, as if trying to determine if I was telling the truth or just saying it to get laid. Quickly satisfied, she pressed her lips to mine again and started tugging up my t-shirt. I pulled my hands from her ass and tugged the shirt over my head. She did the same.

Her beautiful breasts bounced as the shirt came off her head. Her breasts were full and round and milky white. Her areolas and nipples were like dark strawberries on two porcelain plates.

My hands went to her breasts and gently massaged them as my fingertips teased her nipples.

God I loved those big, natural breasts…

Nothing felt as good in a man's hand as a woman's natural tits.

Okay, fine, I like the fake ones, too, but Candice's were freakin' amazing.

My cock was hard and ready to play.

It pushed against my jeans as she slid her ass and cunt back and forth against my thigh.

I put my hands on her ass again and lifted her up as I got out of the chair.

She wrapped her legs around me and I carried her to the bed.

CHAPTER TWELVE: Candice

"Oh, my god, Candice Carlson. What are you doing?"

It was the little voice in my head that sounded like my mother.

"I'm getting laid, mom," the little voice that sounded like me replied. Wait. Of course it sounded like me. It's my voice. Duh.

"You can't do that, Candice. Not with him."

"Yes, I can, mom. Just watch me. I mean, no mom, don't watch, ooh, gross...

"You'll regret it."

"I know, mom. Now fuck off!"

I could feel Tanner's hard cock beneath me as I squirmed against his lap. My lips were locked on his. My fingers were in his hair. His hands were on my ass.

He picked me up as I were light as a feather and carried me to the bed. He set me on the edge of the bed, then pushed my shoulders back. He eased the boxer shorts down my legs and tossed them aside. With his hands on my knees, he spread my legs and smiled when he saw how wet I was.

That's another side note about being a virgin for you: it's like freakin' Hot Springs, Arkansas down there all the time. My pussy was so wet I could feel hot juices running down my taint and into my asshole, like a hot mountain stream.

Tanner kept his hands on my legs as he got to his knees. My cunt was at the edge of the bed. He slid his hands slowly down my thighs.

I held my breath in anticipation of the first hand to touch my clit that wasn't own.

The second Tanner's thumbs brushed against my clit hood my entire body shook, as if I was having a spasm. But it wasn't a spam. It was the first shudders of an orgasm that had been building inside of me for years. It had waited patiently in my womb since puberty, like a dormant volcano waiting for the elements to demand its eruption.

I sucked in air through my teeth and cupped my breasts together. I squeezed my nipples as Tanner's fingers explored the folds of my pussy.

"Beautiful," I heard him say as he bent his head to place gentle kisses on my pussy lips. His lips found my clit and another shudder rumbled through me. My pussy was flowing as Tanner's lips and tongues swirled around my clit and his fingers found my opening. I felt him slide in one finger, then two. His hand was lubricated by my juices. His fingers slid in easily. There was a little pain, but I tried to ignore it.

Nothing was going to stop me from having Tanner's cock inside me. Nothing.

I felt the orgasm building from deep within my body. Tanner quickened the pace of his finger-fucking as he sucked on my clit like a Tic Tac (don't you just love these drunken sex analogies?).

"I'm... cumming..." I said, squeezing my breasts until they ached. "Oh... my... GOD..."

I bucked my ass off the bed and pressed my pussy into Tanner's face. He slid the fingers out of me and covered my pussy with his mouth. He sucked and licked and swallowed and moaned until I stopped thrashing on the bed and begged him to stop.

"Beautiful," he said again, rubbing my thighs and smiling with a face covered in my tangy sauce. He wiped his mouth on the back of his hand like a man finishing a satisfied meal. He got to his feet and stared down at me as he unbuckled his belt and unzipped his jeans.

"Let me do it," I said, pushing myself up. I dug my fingers into the waistband and pulled the jeans and his underwear down his long legs together. His cock sprang up and bounced in my face.

"Careful," he said, smiling down at me. "You'll put your eye out with that thing."

"Shut up," I said with a grin. I let my eyes go down his body. I couldn't believe how beautiful he was. His chest and shoulders were round with muscles. His nipples were hard like little pebbles. My eyes trailed down his chiseled abs and came to rest at the crop of thick brown curls and the cock that emerged from them. It was long and girthy, thickly veined with a head that mushroomed before my eyes.

I took in a slow, deep breath and wrapped my fingers around the shaft. Tanner sighed as I started slowly pumping my hand back and forth along the shaft from base to head. I couldn't help but stare at it. It was the first cock I'd ever seen that wasn't in a magazine or on a computer screen. And certainly, the first cock I'd ever touched. I loved the way it felt in my hand, so hard, so warm, so long... so... addictive...

Tanner put his hands on my shoulders as I played with his balls with one hand and milked the shaft with the other. When I lowered my lips to give the head a little kiss, his fingers dug into my shoulders and he moaned my name.

He smiled as the head of his cock disappeared into my mouth and my tongue swirled along the underside. I was suddenly glad that I'd watched enough online porn to make most teenage boys blush. Hey, give me a break. When you're a virgin, you have to do research so you'll know what to do if and when the time comes. I'm not freakin' Loretta Lynn, you know. There will be no surprises for me beneath the covers come my wedding night.

"Oh, god, Candice," Tanner said as I quickened the pace of my hand on his shaft and the suction of my lips. "I want you. I want to fuck you. I want to be inside of you."

I let his cock slide out of my mouth and he pushed me back on the bed. He climbed on top of me and kissed me again. A good, long, hard, sloppy wet kiss that made my toes tingle.

"I have to tell you something," I said, whispering in his ear.

"What is it?" he asked as he took my earlobe between his teeth.

"I've never done this," I said.

He propped up on his hands and frowned at me.

"You've never done what?"

"This," I said, gazing into his eyes. "I've never had sex."

He blinked at me for a moment. "You haven't?"

"No, I haven't."

"Well, why not?"

I blew out a heavy sigh that made his hair wave. "I was saving myself." Tears came to my eyes. "How stupid was that, huh. I'm the silly girl who saved herself for years for a guy who broke up with me because his mommy told him to." I closed my eyes and shook my head. Now I'd done it. Talk about a mood killer.

"I'm glad you waited," Tanner said. I opened my eyes to see him smiling softly at me. "But are you sure you want to do this with me?"

"I wouldn't be here if I didn't," I said, sniffing back the tears.

"Do you want me to stop?" he asked.

"No."

"Do you want me to make love to you?"

"Yes."

"Do you trust me not to hurt you?"

My eyes went around his. "Yes."

"Then, shhhh...."

He pressed his lips to mine again. This time the kiss was soft and caring. His tongue slowly went around my lips, then probed inside my mouth to find my tongue waiting.

I spread my legs and Tanner lowered himself onto me. I reached down and took his cock in my hand and guided the head to my opening. He lowered his hips until the head was just about to slip inside me. He didn't take his eyes off mine.

I knew every woman was different. I knew that losing my virginity required that Tanner break through my hymen. I knew there could be pain as he tore through the thin veil of tissue. But once inside, the pleasure would override the pain. At least that's what I was counting on.

"Slowly," I sighed. Tanner slid the head of his cock inside me. I could feel the walls of my vagina contracting around him. He slid in a little more and I felt him hesitate. He had reached the barrier. I licked my lips, took a deep breath, and gave him a nod.

Tanner backed out an inch, then slid inside me in one quick thrust. A moment of pain gave way to an intense feeling of pleasure.

"Yessss," I sighed, wrapping my legs around his waist. "Fuck me, Tanner. Fuck me hard and good."

CHAPTER THIRTEEN: Tanner

A virgin?

Are you fucking kidding me?

Candice Carlson was a virgin?

I didn't believe it.

I'd never met a virgin that could suck cock like that.

Wait, I'd never met a virgin.

Holy shit.

How freakin' lucky am I?

Now, I'm not a complete asshole. When she told me she was a virgin I asked to make sure that she wanted to give her cherry to me. She said she did. Never let it be said that Tanner Wright ever disappointed a lady in distress.

I'm also not insensitive to the inner workings of the female anatomy. Candice told me to go slow, so that's what I did. But once the dam broke, she was like a wildcat beneath me.

She clawed my back as I jackhammered my cock in and out of her. Holy crap... she was tight as a drum. It was as if her pussy had little fingers that squeezed and milked my cock with every thrust.

I braced my palms on the bed beside her and watched her face as the virgin's first real orgasm built in her body. Her beautiful big boobs bounced on her chest. She grabbed them and pushed them together and squeezed her nipples until they turned deep crimson.

Jeez, I had the best view in the house for this one.

I felt my balls begin to tighten as my orgasm prepared for eruption. I slid my cock into her as far as it would go, then back out and in again.

"Oh... Tanner... I'm cumming... cum with..."

She opened her eyes and smiled as she came.

She parted her lips and beckoned to be kissed.

My tongue probed deeply into her mouth as my cock filled her with my hot cum.

She grabbed my ass and pulled me into her as she came.

A few more good thrusts, another shudder or two, and I felt her go limp.

With a happy sigh, I collapsed on the bed beside her and fell fast asleep.

CHAPTER FOURTEEN: Candice

The five days we spent in Tucson were the best five days of my life. Not because the work was fulfilling or because I impressed the heck out of everyone with my knowledge of the telecom industry and cost analysis – which I did - duh.

The five days were amazing because they included four nights that found Tanner Wright in my bed.

Even though we could barely keep our hands off one another, we somehow managed to keep our affair a secret.

There was one close call when we were making out in the hotel elevator and Costas and Stan were standing there when the doors opened. Of course, by then, I was on one side of the elevator and Tanner was on the other. We did our best to pretend that we could barely stand one another.

It was one of the hardest things I'd ever had to do. When we were in the same room (or elevator) my fingers longed to touch his skin. My lips ached for his. My lady-parts wanted to party with his man-parts. And party, we did.

We avoided each other during the day, which wasn't terribly difficult. I was always locked away with geeks and analysists while Tanner was wined and dined by the CEO and other executives. I got the distinct impression that if Wright Enterprises didn't acquire Anderson Telecommunications, Anderson would not be around for very much longer.

I spent as little time as possible with the Goldman team, mostly having working dinners in the hotel restaurant to discuss the status of the due diligence we were conducting.

Bob, the forensic accountant hadn't found anything out of the ordinary.

Neither had Irving the attorney or Juliette the... hmm... what was is that Juliette did again?

Stan seemed pleased with our progress and said we'd be flying back to Chicago on Friday. We'd readjourn at Goldman on Monday and take the week to prepare our findings to present to Wright the following Friday.

"I think they're very happy with our work," Stan said smugly, as if the credit was his and his alone. "Let's finish strong, people, and impress the hell out of them next week."

Tanner came to my door every night around ten. He'd slip inside the room, then slip inside me. We alternated between mad, passionate, almost-rough bouts of sex, and softer, gentler, slower, longer bouts of love making.

I can't say that I preferred one over the other.

I loved it all: fast, slow, hard, soft, rough, tender...

I was happy so long as Tanner was beside me.

I was especially happy when he was inside me.

Insert big smiley face...

* * *

Friday morning I awoke to find Tanner sitting on the foot of the bed lacing his tennis shoes. He had left my room early every morning to sneak back to his suite to shower and change for the day.

"Morning," he said with a smile. He leaned over to give me a kiss.

"Morning," I sighed. I picked up my phone to check the time. "Damn, is it Friday already?"

"I'm afraid so."

"Are you flying back with us today?"

"I'm afraid not," he said, shaking his head. "Henry left a text early this morning. I have to fly to Atlanta for a few days to take care of some business, but I'll be back in Chicago for our wrap up meeting next week. I'll text you from the road. Don't worry."

"I'll miss you," I said, trying not to sound like a whiny, clingy girl; which was exactly how I felt.

"I'll miss you, too," he said with a sleepy smile. He leaned down and kissed me again. Just a little longer this time. A little deeper.

Without another word, he crept from my room and left me wondering what our relationship was going to be like once we were back in Chicago.

It was something we hadn't talked about, but something that was always on my mind. I'm a girl, for petesake. That's how we roll. I'd really like to know where I stood with Tanner, but I was hesitant to bring it up so quickly.

Did he really like me?

Or was this just an out of town fling?

An extended one-night stand?

Did we have a future together?

Did I save myself for Mister Right or Mister Wrong?

Did I sound like Lizzie Lohan in a shitty teenage chick-flick?

Yes, the little voice in my head said.

Yes, yes you do.

I tossed my phone on the bed and rolled over to go back to sleep.

I'd drive myself crazy with doubt and pity later.

CHAPTER FIFTEEN: Tanner

When I boarded the plane, Henry Costas was already sitting in his first-class seat on the commercial flight that would take us from Tucson to Atlanta. I had decided to leave the Gulfstream in Tucson for Candice and the Goldman team to fly home on.

It never occurred to me that my undercover act of chivalry would raise any kind of suspicion with Henry.

Obviously, I was wrong, because he was loaded for bear the moment I sat down.

He leaned over to ask, "Tell me again why we're not on the Gulfstream and the Goldman group isn't flying back commercial?"

I gave him a confused look. "You're always on my ass about treating people more professionally and not acting like such a rich douchebag. I thought it was a nice gesture. I thought you'd be proud of me for putting others first."

Henry snorted a laugh. "Give me a break, Tanner. You just didn't want your new girlfriend to have to fly back to Chicago in the back of a plane wedged between those two idiots, Bob and Irving. Very chivalrous of you, my boy. And very out of character."

I feigned ignorance. Badly. "What new girlfriend?"

"Oh, for petesake, Tanner, the girl you've been screwing every night since we got to Tucson." He crossed his legs and brushed a hand over his knee. "Honestly, I thought she was the one woman who wouldn't fall for your tricks. I thought she was better than that." He gave me a sideways glance. "Turns out, she was just another brick in the wall."

"What does that mean, Pink Floyd?"

"It means that you've proven once again that you can get any woman in your bed. Bravo. At least it wasn't an Anderson stock holder or a member of the executive committee. If you had to fuck someone I'm at least glad that it was a junior analyst from Goldman and not someone who actually matters."

I turned sideways in the seat to face him. "That's not what this was."

"No? That's what it looked like to me."

I ground my teeth for a moment. "Wait, how do you know I was with her every night? I was very careful not to... You had me followed?"

Henry blew out a bored sigh and spread his hands. "I had you followed."

I felt my blood boil as I glanced around the cabin to see who might be witness to the fit I was about to pitch. The flight attendants were milling about as the last passengers got situated. Although I was fit to be tied on the inside, I forced myself to remain calm on the outside.

"Why would you do that?" I quietly asked. "Have me followed?"

He looked at me as if I'd asked a silly question. "You're seriously asking me that?" He shook his head. "Tanner, I love you like a son, and I think you're a brilliant guy, but if you spent as much time thinking with your brain as you do with your dick, Wright Enterprises would be a much larger company."

I blinked at him. I loved Henry like an uncle, but I didn't much like him at the moment.

"Maybe you think the company would be better off with you in the CEO chair," I said. "Someone who thinks with their brain because their dick no longer works."

"This is not about me replacing you, Tanner."

"Then what is it about, Henry?" I asked, louder than I should have. One of the flight attendants started toward me, but I waved her away.

"You know what it's about," he said.

"Let's pretend I don't. Tell me."

Henry tugged his reading glasses from inside his jacket and cleaned them on a handkerchief. He set the glasses on the tip of his nose and picked up the copy of *The Wall Street Journal* that had been lying in the seat beside him.

"It's about your inability to see what's right in front of your face, my boy," he said, lifting his chin to peer through the glasses as he scanned the front page of the paper. "Your desire to fuck and party and constantly be the bad boy is blinding you from what's really important. As usual."

I blinked at him and resisted the urge to rip the goddamn paper from his hands. "What am I not seeing, Henry?"

He looked at me from over the top of the reading glasses and sighed. "I'm just saying that if your girlfriend fucks up this acquisition for us, you have no one to blame but yourself. Now buckle up, son. It's going to be a bumpy ride."

CHAPTER SIXTEEN: Candice

I hate to admit it, but knowing that Tanner was now thousands of miles away brought a sense of clarity to my brain, which had taken a back seat to the rest of my organs as of late.

It's hard to focus on mountains of financial data when you're picturing a guy munching on your rug, if you know what I mean.

I spent the weekend reviewing my findings from the Tucson trip and compiling the data into a report that I'd present to Stan on Monday. Anderson's fiber optic expansion plan was sound, albeit it a bit ambitious in the current market. It wasn't something that would affect the deal, just something Wright Enterprises should keep in mind going forward.

As I scanned over the costs associated with the expansion once more (I am a notorious triple-checker), my mind kept going back to the red flags I'd spotted on the older profit & loss reports the first time I'd reviewed them.

Part of the reason Anderson Telecommunications didn't meet market estimates for revenue during those years was attributed to the cost of replacing older networks in the more rural areas the company served.

If the numbers I saw were indeed correct, and Anderson lost money during those periods, the balance sheet that they were presenting today would be inaccurate.

In fact, it could have been off by as much as a hundred million dollars. And if that was truly the case, the stock that Tanner would pay $31 per share for was worth more like $10 a share. If the SEC, the government, or a vested third party ever audited the older books, the discrepancies would come to light and Wright Enterprises' stock could drop like a hot rock.

I pulled up the old P&Ls again, the ones that Henry Costas said were incorrect. I chewed on my thumbnail and went through the numbers again and got the same result.

The difference between what Anderson's current balance sheet showed, and what the historical P&L's showed, was too wide a gap to be missed by Tanner's in-house people. Surely, they went back to investigate it.

Maybe that's when the P&L's were updated and I just didn't get a new copy.

Either the numbers were wrong to begin with and were corrected after the mistake was found; or the numbers were correct in the first place and adjusted to show otherwise.

One, was incompetency.

Two, was highly illegal.

I stared at the screen for a moment, then a thought hit me. I picked up my phone and found the contact information for Ruth Bennett, my personal financial advisor. I didn't have much money for Ruth to manage yet, but she knew I would someday, with any luck. It was the Sunday afternoon, so I called Ruth's home number.

"Well hi, Candice," Ruth said happily. When you manage other people's money, you're always happy for some reason. Even when they call you on a Sunday. "What can I do for you?"

"Hey Ruth, I just had a quick question about the stock of a company I'm consulting with. I apologize for calling you on the weekend, but I just needed to pick your brain if you have a moment."

"Sure," Ruth said. "What's the company?"

"There are actually two companies," I said. "Wright Enterprises and Anderson Telecommunications."

Ruth put me on speakerphone. I could hear her typing. "Okay, Wright stock closed at $97 per share on Friday. The stock is trending up on the news that Wright is acquiring, ah, Anderson Telecommunications."

"And what about Anderson's stock?" I asked. "I assume its ticking up in anticipation of the takeover."

She tapped on the computer keys. "It was up 2% of Friday at $29 per share. It looks like Wright is offering $31 a share, so the Anderson stock holders must be thrilled."

"I'm sure they are," I said, resting my chin on my hand as I stared at the numbers on my screen. "Ruth, what would happen if Wright acquired Anderson, then some issue came to light that showed Anderson's stock was not worth what Tanner, I mean, Wright, paid for it?"

Ruth took me off speaker phone. Her voice was clear when she asked, "Why would you ask that question, Candice? Is Goldman consulting with Wright on the acquisition?"

"I really can't say anything more," I said. "Just tell me, what would be the repercussions if something like that happened?"

She sighed in my ear. "Well, if it comes to light that Wright overpaid for Anderson, both company stocks will plummet. The SEC and the state attorney general would launch an investigation and if anyone is found guilty of cooking the books or doing anything to falsely inflate the stock price, well, people could go to jail. At the very least, the fines could run into the hundreds of millions of dollars."

I felt the breath catch in my throat.

"Candice? Are you there?"

"Yes, sorry. Um, one last question. And this is completely hypothetical. Why would someone do that? Cook the books to inflate a stock price before an acquisition?"

"There are a variety of reasons why someone might do that," she said with an edge to her voice. "All highly illegal."

"Like?"

"Like trying to make the deal look better than it really is. Or trying to make the company appear more sound than it really is. The best reason I can think of is if they were propping the company up so they could later knock it down. They would short both company stocks and when the stocks collapsed, they would make a fortune in the bargain."

I chewed at my bottom lip. "Forgive my ignorance, Ruth, but can you explain to me what you mean by 'short both company stocks'?"

"Basically, shorting a stock means that you are betting against the stock price going higher. You're betting that it's going to go lower in the future. You buy options called 'puts' that give you the right to purchase shares of stock at one price and sell it when the stock reaches a strike point. If you are shorting a stock, you option the stock when it's at the higher price, and when the stock drops, you sell back the option and your profit is the difference."

"So, if someone shorted Wright's stock at $97 per share, with a strike price of say $57..."

"They would see a profit of $40 per share." Ruth was quiet for a moment. "Candice, is there something going on that you're not telling me?"

"No, Ruth, of course not," I said, hoping I sounded convincing. "I'm just on the team doing due diligence for the acquisition and I have to look at every angle. That's all. Just running hypotheticals through my head."

"Well, that's good to hear, dear," she said with a sigh. I could tell by her tone that she was concerned that I was into something I shouldn't be. She drove the point home by adding, "Because anyone involved in that kind of collusion and stock manipulation could go to jail."

"Thanks, Ruth," I said. "That's good to know."

CHAPTER SEVENTEEN: Candice

I spent the rest of Sunday finalizing my report for Monday's wrap-up meeting with Stan and the rest of the Goldman team. The discrepancies in the old P&Ls kept nagging at my brain, but I managed to brush them aside long enough to finish the report.

The report was all sunshine and unicorns.

There was nothing there that would cause an issue with the acquisition going forward.

The red flags had been lowered, now it was full speed ahead.

I patted myself on the back for a job well done.

The one thing I couldn't brush aside was the fact that I missed Tanner terribly. I was amazed at how close I felt to him after our brief time in Tucson. I'm not saying that I'm in love, mind you. I'm just saying that he was constantly on my mind. I hoped that I was on his mind, too.

We didn't talk at all over the weekend, but I knew he was super busy in Atlanta. And the undefined status of our relationship prevented me from calling him every two minutes like I was dying to do. I didn't want to frighten him away, but I didn't want him to think that I didn't want to hear from him either.

It was the age-old single girl dilemma.

Do I call him or wait until he calls me?

But what if he doesn't call me?

What do I do, oh dating gods?

What do I do?

I decided that it was within modern dating etiquette to send a few short texts, adequately spaced out over the weekend so I wouldn't sound too needy.

His responses were short and to the point.

Super busy.

In meetings.

With Henry.

Getting lap dance from stripper ...

Getting blowjob in limo ...

Okay, I made those last two up, but sometimes that's where my jealous imagination ventured. I forced those thoughts out of my head and focused on work.

Tanner would call soon. I just knew it.

I'd hear his voice and know everything was all right.

I went to bed around midnight on Sunday with all my work done. The wrap-up meeting with the Goldman team was at ten the next morning.

I was going to knock their socks off.

* * *

I dropped my purse and briefcase behind my desk, then pried the lid off the cup of black coffee from the shop downstairs and fired up my computer.

Immediately, a message from Stan popped onto the screen.

Please come to my office as soon as you arrive. Stan.

I sipped the hot coffee and stared at the message for a moment. It wasn't unusual to have inner-office messages waiting for me when I arrived, but this one popped up even before I was logged into the company network.

I slowly lowered the cup to the desk and clicked the login button on the screen. My fingers trembled as I typed in my user name and password and hit Enter.

I swallowed the lump that was in my throat as I read the words that flashed back at me from the screen.

Account Restricted. Contact System Administrator.

"What the fuck..." I typed in my user name and password again, pounding my fingers against the keys as if I thought that would do the trick. It was like hitting an elevator button over and over thinking it would get the elevator there faster.

I held my breath and hit Enter.

Account Restricted. Contact System Administrator.

I slowly withdrew my hands from the keyboard.

My fingers curled into my palms.

My heart began to race.

I struggled to keep the tears from welling in my eyes.

I knew exactly what was happening.

My god, how could I have been such a fool.

* * *

When I got to Stan's office, his secretary escorted me to a conference room. She ushered me in and closed the door.

Stan was sitting at the conference table with his hands folded neatly in front of him. He had a nervous look on his face. He motioned for me to sit across from the table from him.

There was a sour-looking older lady sitting next to Stan.

Next to her was serious-looking man with salt and pepper hair and a Brooks Brothers suit.

I pegged them immediately.

She was from human resources and he was from legal.

They were all there to fuck me. And not in a good way.

Stan introduced them as if we were meeting at a cocktail party. "Candice, this is Mrs. Nelson from Human Resources and Mr. Griffin from our legal department. They both looked at me without saying a word.

"What's up, Stan?" I asked, forcing a smile that didn't want to be there. Stan cleared his throat and clenched his hands together until the knuckles turned white.

"Candice, it's come to our attention that during your trip to Tucson you engaged in certain activities that... well... quite frankly, are not acceptable as proper conduct for a Goldman & Stern employee."

There it was.

I had literally fucked my way out of a job.

I tried to hold the smile, but it was no use. It melted from my lips like a snowman on a hot day. I did the only thing I knew to do. I played dumb.

I said, "I'm not sure I know what you're talking about."

The lawyer chimed in. His tone was brisk, like a prosecutor questioning a witness. "Miss Carlson, while you were in Tucson did you engage in sexual relations with Tanner Wright, CEO of Wright Enterprises?"

I suddenly knew how Bill Clinton felt when he was caught banging Monica Lewinski in the oval office.

I did not have relations with that woman, Miss Lewinski...

"I'm sorry, I don't understand why that's anyone's business..."

"It's a simple question, Miss Carlson," the lawyer said with a dismissive shrug. "Did you or did you not have sexual relations with Tanner Wright, CEO of Wright Enterprises and a client of Goldman & Stern, while you were in Tucson. Just answer yes or no."

I blinked at the woman from HR. She was looking at me like she'd caught me banging her husband in her bed. It was a look of disgust and disbelief.

I leaned in to her and said, "Do I have to answer these questions? Don't I have rights under the EEOC or something?"

"I'm afraid the Equal Employment Opportunity rules are not pertinent in this situation, Miss Carlson," she said, looking down her nose in judgment at me. "Just answer Mr. Griffin's question, please."

I glanced at Stan. He was studying his hands on the table. He wouldn't look up at me. I set my jaw and looked directly at the lawyer.

I said, "Yes, while I was in Tucson I was involved in a personal relationship with Tanner Wright."

The lawyer's eyes went around my face. I could see the corner of his mouth twitching. This was kind of turning him on a little. Douchebag.

He said, "You were involved in a sexual relationship."

"Yes."

"Yes what, Miss Carlson?"

I took a deep breath as my career vanished before my eyes.

"Yes, Mr. Griffin. While I was in Tucson I was involved in a sexual relationship with Tanner Griffin, CEO of Wright Enterprises." I gritted my teeth at him. "Is that good enough for you."

"It is," Griffin said with a nod.

"In that case, we have no choice but to terminate your employment immediately and have you escorted from the building," the HR lady said. She blew out a heavy sigh, as if she'd been holding her breath the entire time.

"Stan, you can't let them do this," I said, desperation creeping into my voice. "I'm the best analyst you have. Stan? Talk to me."

Stan finally looked up and shook his head. It was that moment that I knew all was lost.

"I'm sorry, Candice, but your actions have put Goldman & Stern—and our relationship with Wright Enterprises – in a very precarious position. I'm afraid there's nothing I can do."

The lawyer stood up and opened the conference room door. A burly security guard was standing at parade rest outside the door.

The lawyer nodded to me and said, "Escort Miss Carlson to her desk and see that she retrieves only her personal property, then show her out of the building."

CHAPTER EIGHTEEN: Tanner

I felt like a total douchebag when Henry told me that Goldman had fired Candice because of our affair. I felt like a douchebag because I knew ahead of time that she was going to get fired and I didn't do a fucking thing to stop it or to warn her.

Jesus, what an asshole I was!

That sort of thing wouldn't have bothered me a bit before I met her. Now, it ate away at my gut like a cancer.

I also knew that Henry was the one who demanded she be fired. I was livid at first, but finally came to see that he was right: I had to stop thinking with my cock and start thinking with my brain.

I liked Candice a lot – AN AWFUL LOT—but if news of our relationship came to light, it could create the appearance of impropriety that could kill the Anderson deal.

As Henry so aptly pointed out, the financial news media would have a field day. "I can see the headlines now," he said, holding his hands in their air with thumbs touching. "Billionaire playboy fucks management consultant doing due diligence on a major acquisition. Click here for all the juicy details."

"You're overexaggerating," I said, sitting next to him as the plane circled the Atlanta airport. "That won't happen."

"Don't kid yourself. The financial press loved this sort of dirt. They call it hot sex and cold hard cash." He blew out a long breath and gave me a sideways look. "Tanner, you know I'm right."

I knew he was right, but that didn't make things any easier.

"So, what do you want me to do?" I finally asked in defeat.

"First, you have to break off all communications with her. You can't text her, you can't call her, you can't Facebook her, and you sure as hell can't send her Anthony Weiner dick pics. None of your usual stuff."

"Okay."

"And if she tries to contact you, you have to ignore her. Do you understand? Block her from your phone and have no further contact with her."

I had my phone in my hand. I had been holding it in anticipation of the plane landing. The first call I had intended to make was to Candice. It was a call I wouldn't be making. I glanced at Henry and gave him a nod. "Okay."

He put a hand on my shoulder and gave it a shake. "Don't look so down, Tanner. After we close the Anderson deal you can go back to fucking anyone you like. Well, anyone except Candice Carlson."

CHAPTER NINETEEN: Tanner

I couldn't bring myself to immediately block Candice's number, nor could I just instantly banish her from my mind. I replied to a few innocent texts, claiming to be too busy to chat.

Then Henry caught me reading a text during a meeting while he was speaking. He simply reached down and plucked the phone from my hands without skipping a beat. He tucked the phone in his jacket pocket and went on with the meeting as if nothing had happened.

I felt like a child who'd had his favorite toy taken away in front of the whole class.

And without Candice in my bed and in my arms, it was a very lonely, sleepless week.

We arrived back in Chicago on Friday morning. The Goldman team – without Candice – was waiting in the conference room for us after lunch.

"Stan, how are you," Henry said as we entered the room. He shook hands with Stan and the other three stooges. I took a seat and squeezed the red rubber ball between my hands.

"We're all good, Henry, thanks," Stan said in his obnoxious, over-eager manner. "And I think you'll be very pleased with our report." Christ, this guy needed a fulltime assistant just to keep the brown wiped off his nose.

"We're eager to see the report," Henry said, rubbing his hands together eagerly. "This is the last box to be checked before we sign the final acquisition papers on Monday. If Anderson gets a clean bill of health from you, we're all set."

Stan leaned over the table to pass out the perfectly-bound copies of Goldman's report. He sat down and opened his copy, and waited for the rest of us to do the same. I didn't bother looking at it. I didn't want to touch the fucking thing.

That report, and my own actions, had ruined Candice's life. And there was no one to blame but me.

If I had just listened to Henry, if I had just kept my dick in my pants, Candice would be sitting across from me now, pretending to ignore me.

"So, let's begin with our review of the financials," Stan said, flipping through the report. "That starts on page 5."

Before he could continue, the conference room door opened and a large black man wearing a dark suit and tie appeared. Behind him were two other men who sported equally-serious looks on their faces. Behind them was a woman with a short-cropped haircut and a pinched face. I immediately took her as someone from the government.

"What the hell is this?" Henry asked.

The first man held up a badge that made Henry's mouth clap shut. "I'm Agent Richter with the FBI. These are my associates, Agents Brent and Kline. And this is Helen Walters from the Securities & Exchange Commission. We're looking for Henry Costas and Tanner Wright."

"I'm Henry Costas," he said. Henry glanced at me. "This is Mr. Wright. What's this about?"

The FBI agent pulled a folded sheet of paper from inside his jacket and handed it to Henry. Henry opened the paper and scanned it without his glasses. The color drained from his face.

The G-man said, "Gentleman, we have a warrant to seize all files and documentation from these offices and your personal possession pertaining to the pending acquisition of Anderson Telecommunications by Wright Enterprises."

"For what purpose?" Henry said. He glanced at me again. I'd never seen him look so nervous. His reaction to this little raid was interesting, to say the least. I sat back and crossed my arms over my chest and kept my mouth closed.

The woman from the SEC moved to stand next to the FBI agent. She said, "It has come to the attention of the SEC that an off-shore company called Creative Investment Partners has been buying an unusually high number of put options pertaining to Wright Enterprises and Anderson Telecommunications stock."

"People buy puts all the time," Henry said.

"That's true," she said, "But when the person behind the company acquiring all those puts is an officer of one of the companies involved in acquiring the other, that is called stock manipulation and is against the law."

I tapped the rubber ball to my chin and asked, "And who is this mysterious person behind Creative Investment Partners?"

Agent Smith nodded at Henry. "Henry Costas."

"Our initial investigation suggests that Mr. Costas was buying up large numbers of puts because he expected the stocks of both companies to crash after the news that the financial reports of Anderson had been altered by management consultants from Goldman & Stern."

"What?" Stan looked like he was about to shit in his pants. "We didn't alter any financial data."

"Are you with Goldman & Stern?"

Stan slowly nodded.

"Our suspicion is that Mr. Costas was going to claim that you altered the data in exchange for a large contract to do due diligence on the deal," she said, handing him her card. "We'll need to interview everyone who worked on the project."

Now I understood the reason Henry insisted on hiring Goldman & Stern in the first place. He would need a scapegoat when the shit hit the fan.

Poor Stan looked like he was going to have a coronary. The rest of the Goldman team sat wide-eyed with their mouths hanging open as their eyes darted between one another.

I must admit, I would have enjoyed the show if it hadn't meant that my mentor and best friend was trying to screw me. I swiveled my chair to face him.

"Henry?" I said, the rubber ball flexing in my hand. "Why would you do such a thing?"

"You have the right to an attorney, Mr. Costas," the FBI man said.

"And I have the right to know why he would betray me," I said. "Why Henry?"

Henry looked down and shook his head. "I've been trying to get you to grow up for years, Tanner," he said, rubbing a knuckle under his nose. "I've watched you get rich while the rest of us worked our asses off to build this company. You've made billions of dollars while the rest of us fed off your scraps."

"You've made hundreds of millions of dollars, Henry," I said. "Was it not enough?"

"I'm tired of playing nursemaid to you," Henry said, looking away. "It's time I got what was coming to me."

"Well, I'm pretty sure you're going to get that," I said. I looked at the lady from the SEC. "Can I ask how all this came to light?"

"Our office was contacted on Monday by a Ruth Bennett," she said, reading the name off a notepad in her hand. "She's a money manager with Smith-Barney here in Chicago. She was alerted to potential improprieties in the Anderson books by a client of hers. A Miss... Candice Carlson. Miss Bennett contacted our office and we fast-tracked the investigation given the pending acquisition of Anderson Telecom by your company."

"I assume that acquisition is now on hold?" I asked with a smile, already knowing the answer. Fine by me. I didn't want to buy Anderson anyway. This was Henry's baby all the way, and now I understood the reason why.

She said, "Yes, we have an order from a federal judge halting the acquisition. The SEC and the state attorney general's office will be conducting a full investigation."

"Fine by me," I said. I set the rubber ball on the table in front of Henry. "Here, you might need that." I held out a hand to the feds. "Officers, take him away."

"We'll need you to come down and speak with us as well, Mr. Wright," the SEC woman said, handing me her card. "We have no reason to suspect that you were involved in anything inappropriate, but you'll probably want to bring an attorney along just in case."

"I'll have my attorney set an appointment for Monday," I said, slipping the card into the back pocket of my ratty jeans. "I have something extremely important to take care of first."

CHAPTER TWENTY: Candice

After getting unceremoniously fired and escorted from the building on Monday morning, I immediately tried to call Tanner, but found that he had blocked my number from calling his phone.

I immediately knew that something was wrong.

Tanner might have put on the bad boy billionaire persona to everyone else, but to me, he was just Tanner, the amazing man that I couldn't stop thinking about. The man that made passionate, sweet love to me and in whose arms, I fell asleep every night.

There was no way I was just a fling.

I knew it in my heart.

There wasn't a shadow of doubt in my mind that Tanner cared deeply for me.

And I cared just as deeply – if not more—for him.

I could feel it in my bones.

I flagged down a cab and climbed into the back and gave the driver my home address. I tried Tanner's phone again with the same result.

The little electronic voice told me to fuck off, my number had been blocked.

The voice was wrong.

Tanner would not block my calls.

Something else was going on.

My suspicious mind went into overdrive. It didn't take long for me to realize that Henry Costas was the one keeping us apart. He had blocked me from calling Tanner's phone. He had ordered Stan to fire me.

But why?

How was I a threat to him?

You're not a threat to him, the little voice said.

It's your relationship with Tanner that's the threat.

Henry Costas, you slimy douchebag cocksucker.

I'd had red flags waving in my mind since the moment I met him...

Little red flags waving in the air...

Little numbers flying by...

I slid open the contact for Ruth Bennett and called her office. "Ruth Bennett, please. Yes, it's Candice Carlson." Happy hold music filled my ear for a moment, then Ruth's cheerful voice came on the line.

"Candice? Hi, what's up?"

"Ruth, I may have a problem" I said. "And I need your help.

CHAPTER TWENTY: Candice

"Yes, mom. No, mom. I know mom. No, I haven't found a job. Because I haven't looked. Mom, it's only been four days since they fired me. I know. I should sue. I know. You warned me about men. I know. You told me so. Yes, you did."

My phone was on the bathroom counter and I had the Bluetooth thingamabob in my ear. It was Friday night in one of the biggest cities on the planet, and there I was in my bra and panties, shaving my legs in the bathroom sink.

I know, it was sad, the things you did when you were an unemployed, unattached, single girl in the big city.

You shave your fucking legs in the bathroom sink, you eat a gallon of Haagen-Dazs chocolate chip ice cream, and you cry yourself to sleep watching a rerun of *Bridget Jones Diary* on cable.

I tapped the soap off the razor and picked up a towel to dry my leg. The call waiting tone pinged in my ear. Thank god, a reason to get off the phone with my mother.

"Mom, that's someone calling. No, I don't know who it is. Mom, if you'll let me hang up I'll find out who it is. Okay, love you to. Kisses to daddy."

I tapped the little button on the Bluetooth without looking at the caller ID on my phone.

"Hello?"

"Hi," Tanner's voice breezed softly in my ear.

"Hi yourself," I said with a sigh. I put a hand over my heart to keep it from pounding through my chest. I lowered myself onto the toilet. My legs were shaking. I didn't think I could stand.

I asked, "How are you?"

"I'm fine. How are you?"

I struggled to keep the tears at bay. "I'm okay. I heard about Costas being arrested. I'm sorry if I killed your deal. I had to protect you. I hope you understand that."

"I can forgive you if you can forgive me," he said. "I was a fool to listen to Henry. I was a fool to let him keep you from me. I won't ever let anyone keep me from you again."

The tears began to flow despite my best efforts to keep them locked away.

He asked, "Can I see you?"

I asked, "Yes, where are you."

He said, "In the hallway outside your door."

EPILOG: Candice

Six months later...

I stood at the bathroom sink, wiping steam off the mirror with the back of my hand. My long hair was wrapped in a towel. My naked body was covered with little beads of water that ran down between my breasts and sluiced through my short pubic hair to my clit.

Tanner appeared behind me, naked, wet, hard and ready. He wrapped his arms around me and cupped my breasts in his palms. He began to gently massage my breasts. He brushed his fingers over my nipples. They never failed to snap to attention at the touch of his fingers or lips.

His hot mouth was on my neck. I leaned my head to the side and moaned as he nibbled his way to my ear. I could feel his hard cock pressing into my back as he pulled me against him.

He moved his hips to slide the shaft up and down against the wet crack of my ass. I could feel his balls mashing into me. I could feel the hot juices pooling in my pussy in anticipation of his cock impaling me. I could feel the juice running down the inside of my thigh and thought, what a waste.

Tanner's hands slid down my body and found my clit hard and ready beneath the hood. He rolled my clit between his thumbs and slid his fingers into my folds, working his fingers back and forth, soaking them with my juices.

I reached around and took his cock in one hand and his balls in the other. I gently massaged his balls and tugged on his cock. He moaned in my ear.

"I love you," he sighed.

I opened my eyes to find him staring at me in the mirror.

"I love you, too," I said.

"You do?" he said.

"I do."

"Show me."

I turned to face him. He pressed his lips to mine as my hand slowly stroked his cocked. Our tongues dueled like angry snakes. I rubbed the underside of the head of his cock on my belly, leaving a trail of his salty juice on my skin.

Tanner put his hands under my arms and lifted me onto the sink. With my ass on the edge of the counter, I spread my legs for him and he moved in closer. He hooked his arms under my knees to support my legs and ass. I took his cock in my hand and guided him into me. The head slid inside me and we both smiled.

I braced my palms on the counter top. With his arms under my legs, he lifted my ass off the counter and slid fully into me in one thrust. It pushed the breath from my lungs and made me gasp in the most glorious way.

Tanner slid his cock in and out of me, slowly at first, then a little faster, then a little faster still. His cock and balls were quickly covered in glistening juice that filled the air with the tangy aroma of sex.

We both looked down to watch ourselves fuck. I loved to see his cock sliding in and out of me. He loved to watch my pussy lips grab and hold onto his cock as it slid past them.

This was our favorite position because it gave both of us an amazing view of our carnal connection. It was almost like watching your own porno, only better.

Tanner thrust into me and a shudder quaked through my body.

He was pounding into me faster now, harder.

The slap of our flesh joined the sound of our heavy breathing.

I glanced up at Tanner. Every muscle in his body was flexing.

His head was back.

His teeth were clenched.

His eyes were closed.

He breathed through his nostrils like an angry bull.

"I'm... cumming..." he moaned. "Come... with me..."

I closed my eyes and joined him for the ride.

A few more deep thrusts and Tanner pushed his cock into me as far as it would go and growled as he came.

As he filled me with his hot cum, my own orgasm hit.

I threw my head back and squeezed my eyes shut and felt my entire body shake as the orgasm overtook me and sent me over the moon.

When I was over, we opened our eyes and looked down.

We were a hot mess.

And we wouldn't have had it any other way.

THE END

Don't miss out!

Visit the website below and you can sign up to receive emails whenever Amy Brent publishes a new book. There's no charge and no obligation.

https://books2read.com/r/B-A-GACH-LGPMB

BOOKS 2 READ

Connecting independent readers to independent writers.

Did you love *Filthy Boss*? Then you should read *Filthy Doctor*[1] by Amy Brent!

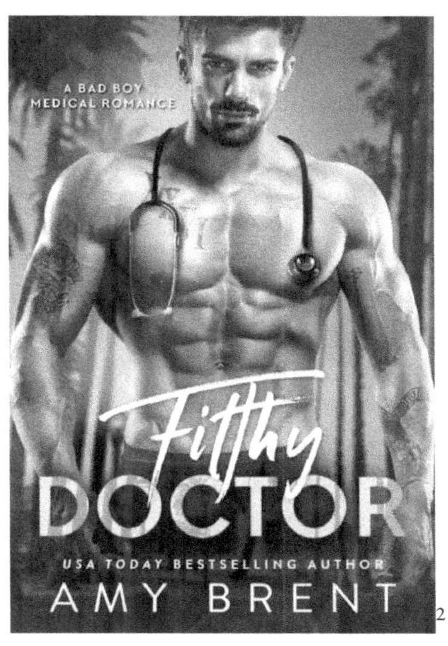

The doctor will see you now... ALL of you.I'm a world-renowned cardiologist, but breaking hearts is what I do best. Women line up for a turn between my Egyptian cotton sheets, making it difficult for me to limit my services to just one. Well, you can't really blame them. Because I work hard, REALLY HARD!With these movie star looks and hands that can work magic - both in the clinic and in the bed, I can make a woman come by just looking at her. And who wouldn't care about a bank account almost as sizeable as the surgical instrument between my legs. Life seems to be awesome. And then Lucy walks back into my world. We were HOT lovers in high school - and I can remember the night I took her V card. Now she's back, as the producer of my TV

---

1. https://books2read.com/u/bPXWk7

2. https://books2read.com/u/bPXWk7

show. My brain tells me to stop.But one look into her sultry blue eyes and I wanna go DEEP! I've learned so many new talents since our last night together, And I am willing to teach her. I'm so ready to be her FILTHY DOCTOR. Her delicious curves tempt me to take her.I want to own that voluptuous body. But doing so would mean risking her career and breaking my biggest rule: Never fall in love.

Also by Amy Brent

Filthy
Filthy Boss
Filthy Doctor
Filthy Professor
Filthy Seal
Filthy Cowboy
Filthy Daddy
Filthy Coach

Forbidded
The Doctor's Fake Marriage

Forbidden
Fake Fiance
One More Chance
Crave Me
My Best Friend's Dad
The Doctor's Fake Marriage
Dad's Best Friend

Forbidden Fantasies
Daddy's Business Partner
Daddy's Friend
Daddy O
Climbing His Corporate Ladder
Taken By Daddy's Boss
Filthy Liar

Standalone
Teachers' Pet
Filthy Box Set
Knocked Up By My Brother's Best Friend
My Best Friend's Brother
My Best Friend's Ex
Say You're Mine
Club Desire Box Set
My Boyfriend's Dad
Fighting For Her
Forbidden Love Box Set
Love Undercover
Friends With Benefits
A Royal Menage
Baby Fever
Vegas Baby
Brother's Best Friend for Christmas
Christmas With My Best Friend's Dad
My Son's Sitter
Single Dad's Christmas Present
Surrendering To 3 Alphas

Because I Love You
Catching Up With Daddy
Claiming Cinderella
Double Trouble
First Love
First Time
Knocked Up By My Brother's Best Friend
My Best Friend's Boyfriend
Pretend Daddy
Redemption
Roomies With Benefits
Royally Yours
Rub Me The Right Way
Show Stopper
That One Night
The Baby Contract
Truth Or Dare
Santa's Naughty List
Quickie on Christmas
Con Man

www.ingramcontent.com/pod-product-compliance
Lightning Source LLC
Chambersburg PA
CBHW071214130726
47998CB00002B/738